SEVEN WENT TO THE COMPUTER PANEL ON THE WALL,

and as she tapped the interface, it exploded, sending her flying backward. She slammed into the wall so hard that the back of her environmental suit made a loud, explosive crack.

Torres crouched. Harry hadn't moved, his boot still in his hand. Ensign Vorik had gone completely flat against the floor, as if he had been hit too.

But Seven had clearly taken the full force of the explosion. The upper portion of her suit was blackened, the faceplate shattered.

The exploded panel exposed sparking and sputtering circuitry in the wall. "Computer," Torres snapped. "Cut power to the wall interface in this room."

With a tone of acknowledgment, the sparks died.

"Harry, see if you can figure out what happened to cause that panel to blow like that," Torres said as she hurried toward Seven. "Vorik, give him a hand."

Seven wasn't moving. Her fractured faceplate made it impossible to get a good look at her face, but Torres could see streaks of bright red clearly through it. She was afraid to risk removing the helmet.

Torres tapped her combadge. "Torres to bridge," she said, "medical emergency. Two to beam directly to sickbay on this signal."

Then she put her hand on Seven's shoulder. "You sure as hell better not die on me," Torres muttered as the beam of light caught them.

STAR TREK VOYAGER®

SECTION 31™

SHADOW

DEAN WESLEY SMITH
and
KRISTINE KATHRYN RUSCH

Based upon STAR TREK®
created by Gene Roddenberry,
and STAR TREK: VOYAGER
created by Rick Berman &
Michael Piller & Jeri Taylor

POCKET BOOKS
New York   London   Toronto   Sydney   Singapore

This book is a work of fiction. Names, characters, places and incidents are products of the author's imagination or are used fictitiously. Any resemblance to actual events or locales or persons living or dead is entirely coincidental.

An *Original* Publication of POCKET BOOKS

POCKET BOOKS, a division of Simon & Schuster, Inc.
1230 Avenue of the Americas, New York, NY 10020

A VIACOM COMPANY

STAR TREK is a Registered Trademark of Paramount Pictures.

This book is published by Pocket Books, a division of Simon & Schuster, Inc., under exclusive license from Paramount Pictures.

ISBN: 0-671-77478-6

First Pocket Books printing June 2001

10 9 8 7 6 5 4 3 2 1

Printed in the U.S.A.

For Val Deaser and Doris Magiera

HISTORIAN'S NOTE

This story takes place some days before the events
of the episode "Equinox."

SHADOW

Prologue

Sloan had been sitting on the couch, in the dark, waiting, for eighteen minutes and twelve seconds. The small crew quarters were cloying, the faint hint of an Earth-based floral perfume reminding him of an interrogation gone bad. The couch was regulation, hard and uncomfortable, obviously little used. An upholstered chair, covered with a knitted afghan, was clearly the one the crewman used regularly.

Sloan had avoided it. She would notice a stranger in her favorite chair, but she might not notice someone on the couch.

It was a test—subtle, but effective, as most of his tests were.

Finally the door slid back with a hiss and the thin, shapely crewman stepped inside. She was alone, as Sloan had known she would be.

"Lights," she said, her voice firm and rich.

As the lights came up the door behind her slid

closed. Sloan had seen pictures of her, but they hadn't done her justice. Her blond hair was long and wavy, pulled up and back to accentuate a beautiful face and dark eyes. She stood five-ten and Sloan knew she was much stronger than she looked. She moved silently and with the grace of a cat.

She was surprised, he could tell, but she didn't even hesitate when she saw him. Instead she kept coming forward with only a nod to him. Sloan was impressed. She hadn't flinched or reached for her hidden weapon. In fact, her reaction to him would not have been noticed by most people. It would have seemed as if she was expecting him. She was good. Not fully trained yet, but still, very good.

"Director," she said, moving around a small dining table to the wall replicator and ordering herself a glass of tomato juice. "I was wondering why I had suddenly been assigned to *Voyager.*"

"*Voyager* has been conducting some antiterrorist operations in the DMZ," Sloan explained. "We need you to collect the intelligence that will enable us to neutralize the Maquis once and for all."

"They're becoming that dangerous?" She turned, glass in her hand, and took a sip, measuring him as if he were nothing more than a target to be shot at.

Sloan smiled. "Let's just say their activities have escalated a little too much to be brushed aside. The political fallout of their actions is already being felt throughout the Federation. Because of the Maquis, our domestic and foreign policies are being called into question at the worst possible time. This area of space is rapidly becoming a military hot zone, and the last thing we need is a bunch of terrorists making an increasingly volatile situation worse."

"So what exactly do you want me to do?" she asked. "I'm being assigned as a computer specialist."

He'd known that. There wasn't much he didn't know. But he let her think she was giving him new information. "Observe and report back."

"Of course." She sounded disgusted, clearly letting him know that she was aware of that part of her job. "What else?"

She didn't have as much respect for him as she should. That worried him, just a little. Still, she was the right operative for the job. How she felt about him mattered less than whether she could complete the work.

Sloan knew she could do that.

"There is nothing else," he said, "unless a circumstance offers itself to you, allowing you to do the work without being discovered. The Maquis threat has to be neutralized, one way or another. More than likely Janeway and *Voyager* will do that for you, but stay alert for opportunities to help the situation along."

She nodded, her dark eyes boring into him as if looking past his blocks and surface protections. A normal person would have been uncomfortable under that stare, but Sloan had seen better and had not broken. Still, he was impressed. Someday, she would be one of his best operatives.

"So you plan to keep me on *Voyager* for a period of time."

"That hasn't been decided," Sloan said. "Stay in a position where you can see and not be seen. Make yourself invaluable to Captain Janeway and that ship."

"Understood," she said.

He stood and stepped toward the door.

"Director?"

Sloan noted that with that one word her voice had changed, becoming softer and much more inviting.

He stopped in front of her, standing easily. He wasn't a large man, but he could intimidate. He chose not to at this moment.

He wanted to see what she would do.

She was shaking her hair loose, letting it fall over her shoulders. Then she smiled. Her hard edges had faded away. The look was seductive, alluring.

"Now that business is over, would you like to stay for dinner?" She gestured at the replicator as she started toward him, her step that of a young girl instead of a dangerous, in-control agent.

Sloan hesitated, staring at the beautiful woman. But his hesitation was playacting, just as her seduction was. He wasn't tempted. He wasn't even intrigued. Seduction had been part of this business for centuries. It was an old trick and the first he had protected himself from.

"I can fix us a few drinks, put on a little music," she said, stopping beside the table, hand on one curved hip. She used light and shadow to her advantage, letting it enhance her athletic, feminine figure. "We can both just relax before this mission starts."

He smiled at her and said nothing. He was impressed how the cold agent who had come through the door a moment before could change to a young, seductive woman without doing anything but altering her voice tones and body posture. Most men would have melted.

"I've got a special program to make a very mean steak and mushrooms," she said, smoothing her uniform with one slender hand. Her fingers lingered just long enough to be noticeable, not long enough to be inappropriate. "And after dinner we can see what happens. What do you say?"

Her smile seemed warm and real. Her scent pulled at him, the perfume mixed with her own fragrance in a way that he no longer found cloying. He noted every detail, storing the information for later. There was no telling when this special talent of hers might come in handy. Seduction was an old trick, but like many old tricks, it had its uses.

"You know that's not allowed," he said. "But thank you for the very nice show. It was entertaining and informative."

For a moment, her face went blank, showing no emotion at all. Then she laughed. The sound was so cold it would have terrorized a normal man.

But he was not a normal man.

Her gaze again bored into him, the seduction and smile gone as if they had never been, her body posture back to what it had been when she entered the room.

He nodded to her and turned for the door. "Good luck on *Voyager.*"

"I won't need luck," she said.

He stopped in the open doorway, the hallway in both directions empty, and glanced back at where she stood. "Just come back with information and we'll see what you need and don't need."

"Yes, Director," she said as the door hissed closed behind him.

He had no doubt that he'd just been tested. She was good.

Very good.

But not as good as he was.

Chapter One

23 hours, 7 minutes

Seven of Nine opened her eyes. Her regeneration was incomplete. Someone had interrupted her. She scanned the darkened cargo bay, her senses on alert. It took her only a moment to spot B'Elanna Torres standing near the alcove's controls.

"Sorry to wake you," Torres said. Like the others on board, she did not properly refer to Seven's regeneration cycle.

Seven did not "sleep" as they did, so the term "waking up" did not actually apply to her. Instead, during her regeneration cycle, repairs were made to her cortical subprocessor, and her day-to-day functions were improved.

Of course, she knew better than to correct Lieutenant Torres. That would lead to an argument—the

7

same argument they had had before, in fact—and that would be inefficient.

"I trust you had a reason for disturbing me," Seven said.

"The captain is intrigued by those two suns that we found. The collision will happen soon, and she wants to divert course so that we can record it." Torres shrugged. "She said—"

" 'How many other starships would get an opportunity like this one?' "

Torres raised an eyebrow. "She spoke to you about this?"

"No." Seven sounded as weary as she felt. "She has said similar things about astronomical events before."

Torres crossed her arms. "You don't agree with her on this one?"

"I believe watching two suns collide will be interesting, but it will also be dangerous. If we are too close . . ." Seven let her voice trail off. Torres knew what would happen. They all did.

"That's why the captain had me wake you," Torres said.

Seven resisted the urge to correct her.

"She wants us to calculate the exact moment when those stars will hit each other."

"I believe you are capable of doing that on your own."

Torres gave her a small smile. "I'll take that for the backward compliment it was."

"You already told the captain that."

"Of course. But she wants more than one set of eyes on this. She trusts yours, for some reason."

The edge was still there. Seven stepped out of her

alcove. She and Torres had reached a kind of peace over the years that Seven had been on *Voyager,* but it was an uneasy peace. They respected each other, but actual friendship between them might never be possible. They could barely have a conversation without irritating each other.

"I shall meet you in astrometrics," Seven said.

"I'll walk with you," Torres said. "I have some figures on this padd, and I'd like to go over them with you."

Seven sighed inwardly. She had hoped for a moment alone. Of course that would not happen. When Captain Janeway wanted something, she wanted it immediately.

She took the padd from Torres's hand and started toward the door of the cargo bay. It had only been two hours since she had entered her alcove. She did not feel as fresh as she should have. She had just entered the most important part of her regenerative phase when Torres had interrupted her. Seven would have to reprogram the alcove next time to compensate.

Torres kept pace with her as they left the control area. "The gravitational fluctuations are severe." She was at Seven's right, leaning in toward the padd. "We'll have to—"

Seven felt the explosion before she heard it. A wave of energy and debris sent her flying across the bay. Then the sound followed, so loud that it felt as if her ears had imploded. Her system registered light and heat and power as she tumbled like a weed in the wind.

The instant stretched into forever, and then to her surprise, she found herself on her back against one of the barrels, her feet twisted beneath her. She did not remember landing.

Her body ached and her ears rang, but she did a quick systems check. Except for scrapes and bruises, she was undamaged.

She used her elbows to prop herself up.

Her section of the bay was ruined. Metal shards and still pulsating chunks of electronics were scattered all over the section. A fire burned where her alcove used to be, and the main control panel looked as if it had melted.

She did not see Lieutenant Torres, but she did see the padd. It had been flat, and now it was L-shaped, as if someone had folded it down the middle.

"Lieutenant?" Seven's voice sounded faint to her own ears. The ringing was irritating. She would have to consult the Doctor about it. "B'Elanna?"

Still no answer. Or if Torres had tried to answer, the ringing in Seven's ears prevented her from hearing it. She pushed herself to her feet, felt new aches in her back and thighs and saw that she was bleeding from a cut along her forearm.

The bay was filling with acrid smoke. Her eyes were starting to water.

"Lieutenant?"

She had to think clearly. She had been standing next to Lieutenant Torres when the explosion occurred. Seven had ended up near a barrel, and the padd had landed several feet away. If the explosive force had hit them equally, then compensating for weight and direction, Lieutenant Torres should have landed equidistant from Seven's right.

Seven turned in that direction, feeling slightly

dizzy. The explosion had affected her balance. Perhaps she was not as undamaged as she had initially thought.

The smoke was getting thicker, and part of the ringing she had attributed to her own ears was actually the sound of a klaxon. The rest of the ship would know that something had happened. Help would arrive soon.

But not soon enough. That smoke was making her lungs burn. She had to find Lieutenant Torres and get her out of here.

A pile of crates had toppled onto each other. They had held herbs, spices, and dried ingredients for Neelix's recipes. Now the foodstuffs were spread all over the floor, along with the blinking electronics equipment and bits of superheated metal.

Seven picked her way across the debris. "Lieutenant Torres?"

Still no response. She pushed aside one of the crates, accidentally sprinkling herself with some pungent Talaxian spice, and then she saw Lieutenant Torres, sprawled facedown, her uniform ripped, bleeding from several wounds on her back. A piece of hot metal leaned against her right arm, and as Seven bent down, she could smell the seared flesh.

"B'Elanna?" she said softly.

The smoke had grown so thick that Seven could barely see. Lieutenant Torres wasn't moving. Seven hit her combadge. She couldn't hear if it made its small chirrup or not.

"Seven of Nine to bridge, medical emergency," she said. "Lock on to this signal. Two to beam directly to sickbay."

11

She was about to give up and pick up B'Elanna in a fireman's carry when the transporter took them.

23 hours, 5 minutes

Lyspa stood in the public viewport, arm around her daughter, Andra. Andra was ten, and had the honor of being the first child born on *Traveler,* although certainly not the last. Population was tightly controlled so that the balance was carefully maintained. Once a death was announced, the next petitioner in line received permission to conceive a new life. Lyspa hadn't tried to have a second child. She had been pregnant with Andra when she boarded the ship, leaving Andra's father behind.

He was dead now.

All those left behind were dead now.

Before her, the blackness of space extended as far as she could see. Pinpoints of light marked the cold unblinking stars that held *Traveler's* future. The future of eight hundred million Rhawns, all bound together in their civilization's greatest achievement—a colony ship. If, indeed, this fragile, cobbled creation they traveled in could be called a single ship.

Behind her, voices murmured as other Rhawns relaxed in the lounge. Vendors sang their wares in harmony and Lyspa knew it would only be a matter of time before Andra asked for a treat.

"How come we can't see it?" Andra asked.

Lyspa looked down at her daughter, at her lavender hair (the color of her father's), her slightly golden skin. She wore a deep purple jumpsuit to accent her unusual coloring—she had learned early

12

that appearances meant everything in their section of the giant ship.

"See what?" Lyspa asked.

"The suns," Andra said. "My teacher says they're going to hit each other really soon now. Shouldn't we be able to see them?"

It was a lesson to her, a bit of history, a cosmic anomaly. Lyspa had kept from her daughter her deepest fears, that *Traveler* hadn't made it far enough outside of the solar system to escape the effects of the collision, that when the suns hit, the energy released would destroy *Traveler* too.

"We haven't been able to see them for a long time," Lyspa said. "Surely your teacher has placed them on the viewer."

Andra nodded. "But it's not the same. How come we can't see them here?"

She had never asked this before. She had never been interested before. Lyspa didn't know if the new curiosity was a good thing or not.

"From this window we're looking toward the future." Lyspa said, amazed that her voice sounded so calm. Inside, her heart had twisted. Memories of a world she had loved were so close she could touch them, of a solar system she had seen both from gray grass of her home and from the cold blackness of space. A solar system and a world long gone. "Out there, we will find a new home."

Andra grunted in disgust. "*Traveler* is my home. I don't need any place else."

Because she hadn't known anything else. She knew the plants of her homeworld because she worked in the gardens, as all of the children did.

13

She had even experienced weather. The sphere had replicated the land as best it could, with streams, and small mountains, and farmland.

But it wasn't the same as having a summer sun against your back, feeling a breeze that brought with it hints of a distant continent, a bit of the ocean. It seemed artificial to Lyspa, and yet it was all Andra knew.

"I want to see the suns," Andra said into her mother's silence.

"I'll pay for some view time later tonight if you'd like," Lyspa said.

"No. I can get that in school. I was just hoping things would change out there." She swept her hand toward the giant reinforced windows, open to the stars. "It never changes out there."

It always changed out there. Lyspa saw the differences every day. Her daughter's comment made her wonder what the school had been teaching.

Or what she herself had been failing to teach.

She had been silent on the subject of stars for too long. Perhaps, after the collision, she would be able to speak of them. Perhaps.

If *Traveler* survived.

22 hours, 35 minutes

"Stop squirming, Seven," the Doctor said, his hand clamped on Seven's shoulder. For a hologram, he had an annoyingly tight grip. "The inner ear is a delicate instrument. Yours has sustained slight damage. If you move in the wrong direction, I may make it worse."

"And then you will correct it," Seven said. "You do not scare me with these exaggerations."

The Doctor sighed. "Just hold still."

She did, although she didn't want to. The ringing in her ears had yet to completely abate, but being in sickbay was getting her nowhere. She wanted to investigate that explosion.

Tuvok was still interviewing Torres. Torres had suffered no inner ear damage, although she had received pieces of shrapnel in her back and legs. She also had taken a hard blow to the head, but, as the Doctor said, if anyone could survive a hard blow to the head, it was B'Elanna Torres.

Seven knew he had not meant it as a compliment. The Doctor hated having an impatient Klingon in his sickbay. And when B'Elanna Torres was sick, she became one hundred percent Klingon.

Tom Paris hovered over Torres, even though his limited medical skills were no longer needed. He seemed at a loss and somewhat disconcerted by Torres's injuries. It was as if he had never seen an injured person before.

"Seven," the Doctor said. "Hold still."

"I am holding still. You are the one who has been moving."

Tuvok was asking Torres the same ridiculous questions he had asked Seven, although he didn't need to use a padd to ask them as he had with Seven. The ringing in her ears had grown so severe that she had to ask Tom Paris if he knew how to stop it. That, in turn, got the Doctor to do more than a cursory examination of her, and he had found the damage in her inner ears.

At least the ringing was diminishing. Now she had to hear those inane questions all over again. Had she seen anyone in the cargo bay who did not belong? Had she noticed any equipment malfunction? Had there been any warning?

If there had been warning, Seven would have gotten them out of the bay. The explosion had happened—as Tom Paris was wont to say—out of the blue.

"There." The Doctor finally put his arm down. "All finished. Although I'm beginning to think I should do something for that neck wobble of yours."

Seven slid off the biobed. "I do not have a neck wobble."

"Yes, you do," the Doctor said. "I think it stems from insatiable curiosity. If I had known you were going to watch everything Commander Tuvok did, I would have faced you in his direction."

Seven raised her eyebrow, giving the Doctor her most intimidating stare. "Commander Tuvok is asking the wrong questions."

"Oh?" That response came from across the room. Apparently Tuvok heard her. "What questions do you believe I should be asking?"

"You should be consulting the equipment," Seven said. "We may have suffered something as simple as a systems malfunction."

"A limited systems malfunction that destroys only your alcove and the board that controls it?" Tuvok asked. "A malfunction that creates a contained explosion which does not damage anything outside of the cargo bay?"

"Do you believe someone deliberately set this explosion?" Seven asked.

"I do not *believe* anything," Tuvok said. "All I have are the facts in evidence. A check of normal systems before the explosion did not show anything out of the ordinary."

"Have you looked in the bay?" Seven asked, remembering the destruction.

"The environmental systems did not respond to the smoke or the fire," Tuvok said. "We had to isolate the bay, then take care of the problems manually before we could send a team inside."

Seven drew herself to her full length. "Have you assembled your team?"

"Yes." Tuvok's gaze measured her. "It is a security team."

He seemed to have anticipated her next question and was letting her know, in his gentle but firm way, that his answer was no.

Still, she had to ask. "I request permission to be on that team."

"Request denied."

"Do you suspect me?"

"No."

"Then I see no reason to keep me off the team."

"Having you along does not follow protocol."

"I know more about that alcove than anyone else."

"Yes," Tuvok said. "And the attack may be perceived as a personal one. I would prefer to have more objective team members."

He nodded at the Doctor and Torres, and then he left. Seven stared at the closing sickbay door.

"Wow," Torres said. "You really pushed him."

"Yeah," Paris said. "If I didn't know better, I would think you almost made him angry."

"My point was not to make him angry," Seven said. "I should be part of the investigation team."

"Well, you won't change his mind now," Torres said.

"That much is clear." Seven strode toward the door.

"Where do you think you're going?" the Doctor asked.

She gave him her most intimidating look again. It irked her that he did not seem affected by it. "Your repairs are satisfactory, Doctor. I am now going to astrometrics, where I have a stellar collision to observe."

"I'll join you shortly," Torres said.

"If you have dizziness troubles, balance problems, or more ringing in your ears, I want you back here immediately," the Doctor said.

Seven did not reply. The sickbay doors hissed open and she stepped through them into the corridor.

The ship smelled faintly of smoke, but she suspected that came more from her imagination than the environmental systems. The corridor was filled with crew members, going in various directions, doing their jobs as if nothing had happened. Normally, she liked this feature of *Voyager*, the way that no event, large or small, could get in the way of the ship's basic functions. But at the moment, it irritated her.

Perhaps Tuvok was right. Perhaps she had personalized the incident more than she realized. Perhaps she was reacting emotionally.

She dismissed that thought. Emotions were irritating. Nuisances. She envied Tuvok his calm and his control. She had to set emotions aside in order to work. Captain Janeway would probably tell her that

18

an emotional response was normal; that she had to experience the emotion in order to master it.

But Seven did not have time to experience the emotion. She had more important things to do.

As she stepped through the doors into astrometrics, she felt her shoulders relax. This place, too, was home. At the moment, it was the only home she had left.

An image of the colliding stars was frozen on the viewscreen before her. She had left it there before she had returned to her alcove. The image was a preliminary trajectory, showing the stars' paths, and then the point at which they would collide. Naomi Wildman had excitedly expressed a desire to witness the event when it occurred.

In fact, the collision wouldn't be as dramatic as it sounded. The stars would sideswipe each other rather than truly collide. But the effect would be catastrophic, as it had already been to the worlds that had once orbited the stars. Gravitational and orbital disturbances had been going on for some time. Chunks of debris from smaller worlds and rapidly dispersing clouds of mostly hydrogen and methane drifted in space where entire solar systems had once been.

Although Captain Janeway wanted precise readings and accurate projections as to the exact nanosecond when the stars would collide, that would have to wait. Seven had other concerns demanding her attention.

She bent over her console and accessed information about the cargo bay. She looked for system anomalies, unusual energy spikes, and evidence of tampering. Then she examined the last readouts from her alcove.

She saw nothing out of the ordinary. But what she

did see catalyzed yet another unexpected emotional response: fear.

If she had stepped off that platform only a few seconds later, she would have died. In fact, if Torres had not interrupted her, the explosion would have occurred in the deepest part of her regeneration cycle, when she would not have felt even a slight energy flux in the system.

Seven of Nine owed her life to B'Elanna Torres.

21 hours, 23 minutes

Emperor Aetayn left his throne and walked to the edge of the control room. He did not pilot this vast ship—this floating world—but he did command it. And with that command came a certain amount of helplessness.

Beneath him, before him, and above him was the blackness of space. Stars streamed past as the tube holding the command center rotated. *Traveler* held over eight hundred million souls, the survivors of a planet nearly eight years gone. The ship itself was a technological marvel. At the time it had pushed the boundaries of Rhawnian know-how.

The ship was over two hundred *triviks* long, made up of six large sections held together—he sometimes thought—by sheer force of will. Each section was composed of eleven tubelike habitat pods—a center tube surrounded by ten others. Each tube spun slowly to create gravity for its inhabitants and to allow plants to grow. Each section was self-sufficient and each mirrored a part of a continent on Rhawn, their homeworld now gone.

Each section held millions of lives, each person going about his business as if he were still on Rhawn, as if this were a normal day.

Aetayn clasped his hands tightly behind his back. But it was not normal. Nothing had been normal since they left Rhawn's orbit ten years ago.

He glanced up. The streaming stars looked the same to him, but his pilots and navigators told him that each time they looked, they saw something different. Perhaps he lacked imagination. Perhaps he was unwilling to see what they saw.

Everything happened so slowly in space.

He turned around. The control room extended as far as his eye could see. His throne rose in the center of it, giving the illusion of power.

He had no *real* power here. If he did, he would force *Traveler* to move faster, to get it out of harm's way. The ship moved too slowly for his tastes. His scientists had warned him that the ship was still too close to the colliding stars, that the *Traveler* would not survive the collision.

They'd done everything they could. For over a century, his people had known about the coming collision. And for that hundred years, they had worked on finding a way off the planet, out of the solar system, to a future somewhere else, somewhere where they could survive. *Traveler* was the best solution they could devise. The entire ship was running on maximum power; every engine, every thruster, every steering jet working to the point of breakdown as they accelerated away from the suns.

But if the latest estimates were true, it would avail them nothing. The ship was still too far inside the danger zone. The blast wave, when it came, would overtake them and rip the ship apart before the remains were incinerated.

Around him, hundreds of Rhawns went about their jobs, monitoring various aspects of *Traveler*'s business. Station commanders stood in front of the sixty-six control panels—one for each tube—and made sure that the information flowed correctly. His navigators made sure they were on the correct track; his pilots kept the various parts of the ship carefully balanced.

No one else seemed concerned. No one except his top-level scientists, who worked in isolation on their own private island in Unit 45.

"Blessed Sky Singers!" Erese, who monitored Unit 3, uttered an oath, breaking all protocol in the command center.

Aetayn glanced at Erese, a tall thin man with graying strawberry hair, and a narrow pinched face. He looked alarmed.

As he did, viewscreens dropped all over the command center. Aetayn hurried back to his throne, only to feel the entire command center shake.

The shake was like a wave fluttering through the ship, as if something had happened farther back, sending vibrations forward.

He glanced at the viewscreen in front of his throne and gasped in horror. An asteroid—a rock no bigger than a boulder—had collided with Unit 3.

The image showed itself on all the viewscreens, the asteroid colliding, disappearing, and then exiting on the other side of the tube.

A tube that held millions of people.

A tube that was now open to the vacuum of space.

Lyspa fell on her back so hard that the air left her body. She skittered across the clear floor, slamming into the trees that had been planted as decoration in the viewing area. The trees weren't upright. She didn't hit the trunk.

She hit the leaves.

The floor was shaking, undulating, feeling as if it were being ripped apart. Screams sounded around her, but they seemed far away. Her ears ached and she recognized the feeling although she hadn't experienced it for nearly ten years.

The pressure in the ship was changing—something that didn't happen in deep space.

Unless there was a problem.

A serious problem.

She reached for Andra, but her daughter wasn't at her side. She couldn't hear her daughter's screams mixed in with the crowds' either. She twisted her head, but she was still sliding on the floor. Beneath her, she could see the stars and something else, something white, something coming from the tube, venting into space.

One of the trees skittered into her and she felt the branches scratch her face. She flattened her hands on the clear surface, trying to stop herself and only partially succeeding. There had been a rupture. Her pilot's training told her that. The atmosphere in this tube would last for quite a while—the tube was huge—but eventually it would disappear.

She had to find Andra.

Lyspa struggled to her knees, only to be rocked

again. This time, she flattened, felt the explosion ripple through the tube. A vendor screamed as his cart fell on him, the electronic heaters flaring brightly. Children's treats—sugar leaves, candy deles, and brightly colored Os—bounced all over the viewpoints. She followed an orange O as it rose in the air and past it, through the clear view wall, she saw more white material venting into space.

"Andra!" she cried.

The shaking continued.

She felt a tug on her clothing, a compelling pull—faint, but insistent. So she wasn't very far from the breach. As the nearby atmosphere vented, the rest would get tugged toward the vacuum, disappearing into the darkness beyond—the darkness that she had grown to hate.

"Andra!"

There was no answer. Other voices called other names. Some voices simply screamed in pain.

But it was her daughter's silence that frightened her.

"Andra!" she shouted again, trying to search every detail around her while praying for a response.

Her prayer was not answered.

Chapter Two

21 hours, 17 minutes

Captain Kathryn Janeway sat in her command chair, staring at the viewscreen. Two stars were displayed on it, impossibly close together, yet not touching, not orbiting. Solar flares arced off them, bright shining orange streaks against the darkness as they ripped at each other. Both suns almost seemed to be boiling, like overheated oceans, their nearness to each other setting off unbelievable gravitational forces that had already ripped apart their planetary systems.

Her bridge crew seemed as fascinated by the image as she was. Harry Kim looked up from his work, as if checking to make certain the suns were still there. Tom Paris occasionally took his attention away from his navigation duties to glance at the orange streaks before them. Chakotay stared at them

DEAN WESLEY SMITH & KRISTINE KATHRYN RUSCH

directly, his fingers templed, obviously lost in thought.

As fascinating as the suns were, she was not concentrating on them. She was thinking about the explosion of Seven's alcove, and the damage it had done. If she hadn't sent B'Elanna to get Seven, Seven would be dead now.

Janeway did not believe the timing of the explosion was a coincidence. Especially since her crew could find nothing wrong with the systems. Nothing seemed to have malfunctioned, and there were no intruders on the ship.

The explosion seemed to have happened for no reason at all.

"Captain?" Harry Kim said. "I'm getting some strange readings."

"In which system, Mr. Kim?"

"Not on *Voyager*."

His words surprised her. She had thought he was searching for the cause of the explosion. She glanced at him. He looked puzzled and focused.

"From something moving slowly away from the two suns."

"What kind of readings, Ensign?"

"A slight energy spike, as if something had exploded."

"On screen."

The image of the suns vanished, replaced by an area of space filled with asteroids. The entire region near the suns was filled with space junk, since the gravitational forces had pulled the two solar systems apart like so much tissue paper.

"Magnify." Janeway stood as if standing gave her

26

a better view of the screen. It didn't, but it helped her think.

The image got larger, showing a long, thin asteroidlike object. Then larger again. What she had thought was an asteroid was clearly constructed. It seemed to be very long and thin and round, like a straw.

"What is that?" she asked, peering forward.

Harry enlarged the image a third time, and this time it was clear. A huge black ship was making its way slowly out of the solar system. Only the ship wasn't all one piece. It was composed of a lot of different tube-like pieces. Ten tubes clustered on the outside, and the eleventh was in the middle of each unit, protected by the other tubes. And there looked to be six different sections somehow tied together.

"Can you enlarge it further, Mr. Kim?"

The image grew one more time.

Each section was composed of tubes that rotated on their own. She recognized the technology from her history. It looked like massive L-5 colonies, O'Neil colonies, once proposed by Earth. Only a few of those had been built and never at this scale.

The ship was huge, ponderous, and extremely fragile. It also seemed to be venting material from one of the sections.

"Is this what I think it is?" Chakotay asked.

"It's a prewarp ship, if you want to call it a ship," Tom Paris said, awe in his voice. "I think a mobile colony might be a better term. That thing looks huge."

"Can you get readings from it, Mr. Kim? Are there any life signs?" Janeway clasped her hands behind her back. Most prewarp ships had little maneuverability and almost no speed. If this thing was full of lives—

"I get life sign readings in the billions, Captain. Over eight hundred million of them are humanoid. The rest seemed to be lower life-forms of some kind."

"An ark?" Chakotay asked softly.

"It would seem so," Janeway said.

"They got that thing out of the solar system?" Paris said, the awe in his voice growing. "It must have taken them years."

"Not to mention all the time it took to build the ship and then to board it." The scale amazed Janeway. She couldn't remember ever seeing anything of this size. It was so big that *Voyager* would look almost like a bird flying down the middle of one of the smaller tubes.

"What's venting?"

"It's not something from the engines," Kim said. "They're attached on the sunward side."

Chakotay was also working his console. "I would have to guess that it's atmosphere."

Janeway let out a small breath. "Can you magnify a final time, Harry?"

Once again the image grew. Then it grew again, until it focused on the area sending plumes of white into space. Two large holes marked the tube near its upper end. One hole had been punched inward, the other outward. The holes were the size of a small house.

"There's an asteroid moving away from the ship," Harry said. "Looks like it punched through the tube."

"They have no shields!" Paris sounded shocked.

"And probably little else to protect them," Janeway said.

"It's amazing they made it this far, then," Chakotay said. "With all the debris around them, they should have been hit long before this."

"Obviously the loss of a single tube won't cripple them," Janeway said.

"But living beings are on that ship," Harry said. "The tube is filled with them."

"Let's hope they have a way to repair the damage," Janeway said. "And quickly. At the moment we're too far away to help immediately."

She glanced at Tom. "Move us closer, Mr. Paris, but keep us out of their sight."

"They have smaller ships gathering around each opening," Harry said.

"At the moment?" Chakotay asked, glancing at her, picking up her thoughts as he often did.

She nodded. "The people who built this ship clearly came from one of those destroyed planets."

"They're all that's left?" Paris ran a hand over his face, as if the idea was too much for him to take in.

"And they seem awfully close to those suns to me." Janeway returned to her command chair. With a sureness born of long practice she called up the preliminary figures on the suns that Torres had prepared for her.

Then she cross-checked the information with the data on the ship, locating its position in comparison to the explosion and destruction area the coming collision would cause.

"Captain?"

Something must have shown on her face, because

Chakotay spoke in his worried voice. She lifted her gaze, met his. For a moment, she let him see the shock she felt. Then she covered it, became the captain again.

"If B'Elanna is well enough to work, I want her to double-check these figures with Seven in astrometrics."

"All right." Chakotay didn't move, didn't relay the instruction. "What have you found?"

She took a deep breath. "If these figures are correct—and I have no reason to doubt them—the suns will collide and explode in just over twenty-one hours."

"The force from that will be . . ." Tom Paris's voice trailed off. He whirled in his chair.

"Unbelievable, yes." She wasn't looking at Paris or Chakotay. She turned her attention back to the viewscreen, to the tiny jet of atmosphere leaking from the tube on the side of that giant ship.

"You were right, weren't you?" Chakotay said. "They're too close."

She nodded. "When those suns explode, that entire civilization will perish."

21 hours, 16 minutes

Traveler continued to shake. If the shock waves were this strong so far away from Unit 3, Emperor Aetayn had no idea what they'd be like closer to the damage. The shock waves themselves were a threat to *Traveler*'s integrity. The units were held together inside the massive structure, connected only by magnetic binding to allow each unit to rotate freely. Too much shaking and the entire ship would just come apart.

"Stabilize the ship!" he cried, and his words echoed throughout the command center.

"The jets have been firing, sir," said Commander Erese. Aetayn knew the jets were designed for just such an emergency—the ship's builders had anticipated more tragedies like this than they had experienced in the first ten years.

Erese went on. "The impact was severe. It will take most of the day to stabilize the ship."

But the waves had eased. Aetayn could feel that. "How is our structural integrity?"

Erese looked toward Iquagt, the operational commander of *Traveler*. Iquagt was a heavyset man whose hair had turned an off shade of violet owing to all the stress of the past few years.

"Structural integrity, sir," Erese prompted.

Iquagt raised his head, his hair falling into his face. He had burn scars along his neck and shoulders, which he'd suffered in an accident two years before, as *Traveler* had passed the last planet in the solar system.

At the time, Aetayn thought he was going to lose Iquagt, but it hadn't happened, and Aetayn had been relieved. Very few people had the focus, concentration, and sheer gall that it took to pilot a ship like *Traveler*.

"Repair crews are responding to the junctures," he said. "Hope we don't need them, because many of our emergency ships are handling the breaches in the hull of Unit 3. This one is serious, Your Excellency."

Aetayn sat down in his throne and studied the viewscreen. He'd purposely blocked out all thought of the deaths that had already occurred. But he would have to deal with them—and all the attendant problems, if the ship survived the next day.

Why did emergencies have to pile one on top of another?

He rubbed his nose with his first two fingers, hitting the relaxation pores on either side of the bridge. The action released mild endorphins that should have elevated his mood and dissipated some of the alarm he was feeling.

But the action created no difference. The sense of impending doom nearly overwhelmed him.

He forced himself to concentrate on the emergency ships, now visible on his viewscreen. The ships had already formed a wedge over the openings and were covering it with a metallic blanket-like seal. There was a name for that stuff, but Aetayn couldn't remember what it was. It had been described to him over eleven years ago; he'd never seen it in action before.

The ships pressed the seal onto the hull, where it adhered to the surface. Once the opening was covered, crews would do the same on the inside and then repair the remaining cracks.

He imagined it as if a small hole had appeared in the corridors near the command center. A hole in the metal, nothing more.

But he knew that wasn't accurate. Unit 3, as all the other units, had been designed to replicate part of a continent and somewhere inside it, some region, some city had just experienced a catastrophic event.

He had to put himself back in Rhawnian mode, and act the way his father had when natural disasters had struck regions of the planet. Aetayn had only been emperor for twelve days when the ship had been completed. He hadn't dealt with disasters, natural or otherwise.

Or at least, disasters that had a direct impact on his subjects on Rhawn, or inside this ship.

He tried not to think about all the subjects who had chosen not to follow him onto *Traveler*. Chosen not to, or had been unable to afford to.

They were over eight years dead. He'd watched the destruction of his home planet on this very viewscreen and imagined he heard the faint voices of his subjects who had decided to remain there, who had hoped beyond hope that the scientists had been wrong, or who had decided that the Sky Singers would save them.

But the Sky Singers had proven themselves to be myths, not gods, and the scientists had been right.

What had it been like in that last year, when the land trembled all the time, when the volcanoes blew and storms covered the planet's surface?

He would know the answers soon enough, he supposed. The slight shock waves that had jolted the command center were just the beginning.

Unless his scientists discovered a way to get *Traveler* to move even faster, these deaths today were just the beginning.

The beginning of the end to his entire species.

20 hours, 55 minutes

The jolting waves had stopped. The floor no longer moved, although she still felt vibrations. The entire unit no longer shook. Lyspa was wedged between two trees, their branches poking her, their leaves covering her face. The leaves smelled faintly of wet soil, reminding her of days she'd spent playing in the forests as a child.

Forests now gone.

She brushed the leaves off her face and sat up. Bruised, scratched, but alive. All around her, people were moving again—if they could. Carts were overturned, food was everywhere, and above her, one of the reinforced clear windows had cracked. Through it, she could see emergency ships drifting nearby.

She glanced at her wrist. Her summons watch had been destroyed. She should have been outside, flying the ships, using all that training—the training she had paid so much for, the training that had, ultimately, gotten her and Andra off Rhawn.

Andra.

Lyspa rubbed a hand over her face, felt the stickiness of blood. She looked at her fingers, saw the deep mauve that indicated she was bleeding more than she should have been, which probably accounted for her lack of concentration. But she didn't feel injured. She sat up slowly, trying to pick her daughter's voice out of the moans and cries.

Nothing.

"Andra?"

Lyspa could no longer see where they had been standing before the accident occurred. That part of the floor was buried beneath chairs and bodies and carts that had slid in that direction.

Bodies.

Lyspa pulled herself out of the trees, scraping her hands on the branches, feeling the scaly bark cut into her skin. She didn't care. She had to find her daughter and she had to do it soon.

The feeling in her ears had eased a little. The pressure inside the section had stabilized—or it had stabilized enough that the environmental systems had come back on, using way too much energy while the tube was repaired. Eventually, it would be self-sustaining again. That was how it was designed.

Beneath the tree's massive trunk, legs stuck out. Legs encased in striped pantaloons, showing that they belonged to one of the vendors. She pushed aside some ripped branches, saw that the vendor's eyes were open and a bubble of blood was on his lips.

He was dead.

She raised her head quickly then, trying to deny the panic welling within her.

"Andra!"

Still no answer from her daughter. Her precious daughter. Lyspa stumbled away from the trees, toward the raised area of the floor where she and Andra had been standing not too long ago.

As she moved, a hand caught her ankle and she nearly fell.

She looked down. The hand was attached to a blood-covered arm which was attached to a blood-covered girl with familiar pale eyes.

"Andra!"

Lyspa crouched. Her daughter's mouth moved, but no sound came out. They had been this close to each other and she hadn't known it.

Andra was alive.

The joy mingled with the all-too-familiar fear. Small burns covered the oxygen holes in her neck, making it impossible to feed air to her voice box. At least her nose was undamaged, and so were the breathing holes on her collarbone.

Lyspa hesitated to touch her daughter, afraid of making the injuries worse. Then she saw the blood smears along the clear floor. Andra had pulled herself toward her mother, probably in response to her voice.

"Oh, baby," Lyspa said, as she examined her daughter. Andra's face was bruised and covered with small burns. Apparently she had been hit with hot *deles* from one of the vendors' carts. They left little square burns all over Andra's body. But the burns didn't look that serious to Lyspa, not incapacitating anyway.

Although her medical training was limited. A yearlong course for pilots, specializing in injuries that could occur aboard small ships, like one of the hundreds of Scouts that clung to the outside of *Traveler* like burrs. One day, she had hoped to pilot a Scout from *Traveler* to a new homeland, ferrying passengers to that new planet as she had ferried them off of Rhawn.

"Oh, baby," Lyspa said again. Her daughter had never been injured before, had hardly ever been sick in her entire life. "Can you walk?"

Andra pointed to her left foot. It was a mass of blood and tissue, with a bit of bone peeking through. Her right wasn't much better. That explained the drag marks. Andra couldn't walk.

Lyspa took a deep breath. Her training had specified calmness. She had to remain calm to take care of a patient, even if that patient was her own child.

She cast about for help, but saw that very few people in the rec area appeared ambulatory. Pots and chairs clogged the main entrance to the viewing area. Obviously they had gathered there when the hull had breached and now that it was sealed—or sealed enough—they had ceased moving.

Lyspa couldn't climb through that entrance with an injured child. Besides, the damage had to be worse there. She glanced at the doors at the other end of the view area. The signs tilted sideways but were still there:

DO NOT ENTER
JUNCTURE POINT
AUTHORIZED PERSONNEL ONLY

Andra caught her gaze and shook her head. Crossing into new sections was completely forbidden without a work visa or special papers. They had neither. And they would be charged with illegal trespass.

"It's an emergency, Andra," Lyspa said. "They should be opening that door any moment."

It was the only way that outside rescue personnel could enter. And they had to enter, once Emperor Aetayn gave them permission to cross the junctures. Each section would have to send aid. That was how *Traveler*'s charter had been set up.

Near the main entrance a woman screamed. It sounded as if she had just awakened and discovered her predicament. But the scream was a single one-shot thing. She didn't cry out again.

Andra looked in that direction and so did Lyspa. A man leaned over the woman. He'd helped her—set a bone maybe, or reattached a dislocated shoulder.

"I'll speak to him," Lyspa said. She kissed her hand and touched it lightly to her daughter's hair, streaked and matted now with blood, then made her way across the rec area.

The floor was still shuddering, but not as bad as before. The movement made her feel unsteady on her feet. So, too, did her own injuries, slight as they were. Amazing how she could have felt so good a moment before and so disoriented now. Until she stood, she hadn't given any thought to the rest of *Traveler.*

She had assumed only Unit 3 had been damaged, but what if units all over the ship had been harmed. What if she took her daughter through that juncture point only to discover something worse?

It wasn't possible. If that had happened, the emergency ships wouldn't have arrived so quickly. Unit 3 was one of the poorer regions on *Traveler.* The ships would have gone to the emperor first, and then to Unit 1, where the council met.

More trees had fallen all along the clear floor, and beneath some of them, she could hear moaning. A steaming pile of Os oozed beside yet another overturned cart, and beyond it, some melting ice was mixing with the blood and goo. Soon this would all start to smell bad—and that wasn't even counting the bodies.

She finally made it to the man and woman. She hadn't seen them before, or perhaps she hadn't noticed them, not with all the other people in the section.

The woman was covered with dirt from a shattered pot that had, only moments before, housed a decorative shrub. She was turning her hand over and over, examining the palm and the back as if it belonged to someone else.

The man stared at her movements, studying them.

He had helped her then. Lyspa tapped him on the shoulder.

He turned to her, his pale peach skin streaked with dried blood. He was covered with scratches just as she was.

"I was wondering if you had medical training."

"I'm interning." His voice sounded hollow, as if he were reciting the part for a play. This hadn't become real to him yet.

"My daughter, she's badly injured and she can't even speak. Please."

"I don't have my equipment. Just my bag . . ." His voice trailed off as he cast around him. He felt the ground, then shook his head. "I guess I don't even have that."

"Please," Lyspa said. "I need to know if I can move her."

That got the woman's attention. She stopped turning her hand and looked up. "That entrance is good and blocked, and I don't think we want to go beyond it. There's emergency ships outside. We can wait for them."

"You can, maybe," Lyspa said. "But I'm not sure my daughter can. Please?"

She looked at the man again.

He nodded, then touched the woman lightly on the shoulder. "Are you up to joining us?"

"It was just my arm, Cyot." The woman sounded annoyed.

He didn't seem to notice. He stood, then helped her up, both of them swaying slightly as they adjusted to the shuddering floor.

Lyspa exhaled, and felt some of the panic leave. It

was better to have another set of eyes on Andra. Lyspa was competent, but competency didn't always work with one's own child. Bias came into play—especially with a child as precious as Andra, the only remaining part of her father, and the only child Lyspa would ever have.

She could see her daughter near the downed trees, propped up on her elbows, watching. Andra looked thinner and younger than she had only moments before. It had to be a trick caused by the blood, the light, and the strangeness.

Cyot walked slower than Lyspa wanted. He glanced at the overturned carts, the ruined chairs, the cluster of trees. "People are trapped."

Lyspa nodded, feeling the panic rise again. "We can help them in a moment. Please. My daughter's vocal airholes are blocked. I'm afraid—"

He put a hand on her shoulder and she winced. He hit a bruise. "I'll help her," he said, "if you help me."

Lyspa shot one more desperate glance at the tilted signs above the juncture doors.

"Of course I'll help," she said, wondering if she lied.

20 hours, 42 minutes

Janeway stopped outside the briefing room door and gathered herself. This meeting had to go quickly. A lot was happening, and she wanted to make certain both she and the senior staff were up to speed.

It always amazed her that the ship could run smoothly for weeks, encounter nothing out of the ordinary, and then—suddenly—everything came apart.

It was as if she were being tested, as if each new obstacle was greater than the last.

Then she smiled. She didn't have the ego to believe she was the focal point of the universe. She had met other captains who did, but she had never been one of them.

And with that thought, she stepped inside the conference room, the door hissing open and revealing her senior staff gathered around the table.

In some ways, she felt more comfortable in this room than she did in her own quarters. Its plush setting and harsh lighting was conducive to creative thought. She had learned a lot here, both from herself and from her crew.

Chakotay sat at his normal spot near the head of the table. B'Elanna sat across from him, Tom Paris beside her. They had been holding hands beneath the table and B'Elanna had pulled away as Janeway entered the room.

Janeway pretended not to notice. Harry Kim had seen the movement, though, and had given Tom an amused look. B'Elanna glared at Harry, but her fierceness didn't seem to bother him.

Tuvok was studying a padd at the opposite end of the table, and Seven stared at him, seemingly lost in thought.

The Doctor was leaning back in a chair, humming. It sounded like Wagner to Janeway's unpracticed ear, but she couldn't be certain. He'd taken to composing his own music lately and it was a bit derivative, although she hadn't told him that.

As she walked to her place at the end of the table, she opened the meeting. "Before we get to our mystery ship, I want to know what caused the explosion in Seven's alcove. Mr. Tuvok?"

Tuvok looked up from his padd. He set it on the table and folded his hands over it so that Seven, who was peering at it, couldn't read it. "Our examination of the area was inconclusive, Captain."

"Inconclusive?" Janeway sat down. "I don't like that word."

"I am simply stating fact," Tuvok said. "The debris held nothing unusual. We found no evidence of a bomb or an intruder."

"I trust you ran a systems check," Janeway said.

"It too was inconclusive."

"Surely you found something, Mr. Tuvok."

"No, Captain," he said. "We did not."

"You're telling me that the alcove simply exploded. There was no reason for it."

"None that we could determine." Tuvok slid the padd closer to his body. "I did ask Lieutenant Torres to assist me after our initial investigation."

Seven raised her head slightly and Janeway thought she noted irritation in Seven's expression. Sometimes it was hard to tell. Seven often looked irritated. That emotion seemed to be the default setting for her face.

"Lieutenant Torres's investigation also proved inconclusive," Tuvok was saying.

"I wouldn't say that." B'Elanna leaned toward Janeway. "We were able to rule out a number of things."

"Such as?"

"A bomb, as Tuvok said. Intruders. A slow systems malfunction. Whatever happened, happened quickly. Nothing out of the ordinary went on before the explosion—at least nothing that our computer records caught. I checked and double-checked the information and I saw no unusual readings."

Seven's lips pursed and her eyes narrowed. Janeway turned to her. "Do you have something to add, Seven?"

"No." Seven's voice was laced with contempt, and she shot a not-so-subtle glare at Tuvok. He didn't seem to notice.

"So what could have caused this?" Janeway asked B'Elanna.

"Several things," B'Elanna said. "Any changes in the regeneration program might have initiated a sequence that was unique to the alcove. We're not completely familiar with Borg technology—"

"I am," Seven said.

"Something seems to be bothering you, Seven," Janeway said. "What is it?"

"Lieutenant Torres and Commander Tuvok seem to believe that this is some kind of strange systems malfunction."

"And you don't?"

"My experiences have taught me to be extremely cautious, Captain. The Doctor insists that he monitor my implants, and I do the same with the alcove. Every night before I go into my regeneration cycle, I run a systems diagnostic. If there was a problem, I would not have entered the alcove."

Janeway stared at her for a moment. Seven seemed more disturbed by this than she was letting on. And who could blame her, after all. This was her private place, her resting place.

"I just said that the problem did not show up in the system before the event occurred," B'Elanna snarled. Tom touched her hand and B'Elanna jerked away, calling more attention to his movement than it deserved.

"Could something have happened that our systems were unable to detect?" Janeway asked.

"Unlikely, Captain," Tuvok said. "That would suggest the presence of some outside force. There is none."

"Except that ship out there." Tom Paris nodded toward the viewscreen.

"With prewarp technology." Harry Kim shook his head. "If they knew how to tamper with *Voyager*, you'd think they'd have built a faster ship."

"We'll get to that ship in a moment," Janeway said. "I'm still unsettled by the notion that we might not pick up a serious flaw. B'Elanna, I want you to run every systems check you can think of down to the smallest level, and then I'd like you to run them again, just to make certain you haven't missed anything. *Voyager* has been traveling now for years without a starbase overhaul. We have to expect strange things to go wrong."

"I didn't get a chance to finish, Captain," B'Elanna said, with a bit too much edge in her voice. "I think we should consider the possibility that this may be nothing more than a compatability issue. Maybe the problem stemmed from a fault in the interface between the Borg technology and ours. The explosion is consistent with an overload, as if our systems couldn't handle something on the Borg end."

"There is nothing wrong with the Borg technology," Seven said.

44

"I thought we set up the alcove in such a way to avoid mishaps," Janeway observed.

"We did." Seven folded her hands in an unconscious imitation of Tuvok's. "Ordinarily Borg technology overrides and assimilates foreign technology, forcing it to conform to Borg parameters. But in order to preserve the integrity of *Voyager*'s systems, the alcove technology was modified to be noninvasive, necessitating the less efficient interface. That's one of the many reasons I ran the nightly diagnostic."

"Diagnostics aren't cure-alls," B'Elanna said, "and there may be an answer in those pieces of the alcove that we haven't investigated yet."

"Well, investigate them," Janeway said. "In the meantime, make sure the other alcoves are safe for Seven to use. She needs downtime just like the rest of us do."

"More," the Doctor murmured. Seven glared at him. He didn't seem to notice.

"That might not be such a good idea," said Torres.

Janeway frowned. "You think the other alcoves may malunction as well?"

"Until we know what caused it, we won't know how to prevent it." B'Elanna sounded surly.

"Are you saying it's not safe for her to regenerate?" Janeway asked.

B'Elanna shook her head. "No. But I think that Seven will need to be cautious."

"I am always cautious," Seven said.

Perhaps within her definition of cautious, Janeway thought. She sometimes seemed impulsive to Janeway. But she certainly didn't want anything to happen to Seven. She had become a valuable member of the crew and along the way, she had become more than a project to Janeway. She had become as important as everyone else sitting around this table. They had come too close to losing Seven for Janeway's comfort.

"Well," Janeway said, "let's make certain that we run extra diagnostics before you use any of the other alcoves."

Seven pursed her lips again and was probably going to inform Janeway that her diagnostics were always thorough, but Janeway jumped in with the next part of the meeting.

"Now, let's discuss that alien ship, if 'ship' is the term we should use. Mr. Paris thinks that the term is inadequate."

"I've seen cities smaller than that ship," Paris said.

"I haven't been briefed on it," the Doctor said. "What ship?"

Janeway suppressed a smile. The Doctor always believed he was behind on everything, even though this meeting *was* the briefing to inform everyone of the ship. "Mr. Kim?"

Harry Kim stood beside the viewscreen, which now held the image of the alien vessel. "It's a pre-warp colony ship," he said. "It consists of six sections and in each section are eleven habitat pods that rotate—"

"We'll get to those specifics in a moment," Janeway said. "The important thing here is that we have found at least eight hundred million sentient life-forms on that ship. They've clearly come from one of the destroyed solar systems. That ship is a last-ditch effort to save their species."

"How could a prewarp culture get that far outside their solar system?" The Doctor asked.

"They're *not* that far," B'Elanna said.

"That's right," Tom said. "Not nearly far enough."

"Then they will perish," Seven said, with her dramatic flair for the obvious. "Unless we do something."

Janeway nodded.

"Captain, if they're prewarp, we can't do anything," Chakotay said. "The Prime Directive—"

"Doesn't apply here, Commander," Tuvok said. "If you recall how General Order Number One is worded, we are unrestricted in these circumstances."

Janeway leaned back in her chair. She had planned on discussing the Prime Directive, but not so soon.

"Oh?" Paris asked. "How do you figure?"

"Among its many particulars, the Prime Directive states that Starfleet personnel may not interfere with the 'natural development of a prewarp society.' This, clearly, is not the natural development of this society."

"You could make the case that it is," Paris said. "After all, the stellar collision that put them in this mess is a natural phenomenon. If they—ah, hell. I can't believe I'm arguing to let all those people die."

"I can't believe you're doing it either." Torres crossed her arms. "This isn't an intellectual exercise."

"Nor are we going to interfere with their normal development," Janeway said. "We're going to enable it. This species has clearly shown its desire to live. It simply miscalculated. Had that ship left their planet a year earlier, it would have survived on its own."

"Maybe it did," Kim said. "Maybe something happened that slowed it down."

"Like the asteroid?" Paris asked.

The crew members who hadn't been on the bridge when the ship was discovered seemed surprised.

"Asteroid, Ensign?" Tuvok asked, showing as much surprise as he was capable of.

"That's how we discovered it," Kim said. "I noticed small explosions that were caused when an asteroid crashed into this section of the ship." He pointed to the damaged tube. The image was taken later than the initial ones, and it showed small ships outside the larger one, repairing the damage. Janeway was even more impressed at how well the aliens had planned.

"I don't understand how something this big could have made it outside a solar system," the Doctor said. "Isn't that why warp technology was invented, to make such travel possible?"

"To make such travel *viable,* Doctor," Janeway said. "It was possible before that, but this is the first culture I've encountered that found such a trip necessary without warp technology. In fact, we could argue— and I probably will in my log—that because this species has ventured so far out of its normal environs, it's at least attempted to prepare itself for the possibility of first contact with another civilization. Within that context, it meets the criteria of a warp culture."

"There is a certain logic to that," Tuvok said. "One cannot assume that every culture will develop in the same way. Some cultures may not ever achieve warp technology while they might achieve its ends. Philosophers within the Federation have argued this part of the restriction for decades now, and have yet to come to a satisfactory conclusion."

"Well," Janeway said, "like B'Elanna, I do not

want to consider allowing this civilization to disappear. We have to find a way to help them."

"That monster ship presents all kinds of problems," B'Elanna said. "It's the most fragile thing I've ever seen."

"How are they keeping that thing moving together?" Tom asked.

"Ingenious thinking," B'Elanna said.

"I'll agree with that," Janeway said.

"From my scan," Kim said, "I've figured out this much. Each habitat pod is connected to the overall superstructure by what appears to be a magnetic coupling that allows each environment to rotate for the gravity inside, yet at the same time keeping it connected to every other tube through a massive, frame-like superstructure."

"How do they propel this thing?" the Doctor asked. "I thought such colonies were supposed to be stationary."

"I think Lieutenant Torres's word is apt," Janeway said. "This is an ingenious system. The aliens have used over three hundred atomic fission engines for propulsion, all bunched in a large unit on the end. Most likely their control room is on the opposite end."

"Primitive sublight technology," Seven said. "I do not know how you can compare it to warp."

Janeway smiled at her. "Maybe because they made it work."

"It shouldn't work," B'Elanna said. "The thrust from those engines on such a massive structure should have caused it to shake or twist apart long before now."

"That was my first thought," Janeway said. "But

they came up with a solution, which I find quite impressive. Mr. Kim?"

"They use thousands of steering thrusters," Harry said. "Positioned along the superstructure, they fire when they're needed to make any adjustments in any part of the ship. The thrusters compensate for the force of the main engines, keeping the ship stable. It's an incredibly complex system, but without the thrusters, the entire thing would have shaken apart before it even got moving."

"They built a spaceship practically out of spit and glue, and somehow they almost got it outside their solar system." Tom Paris shook his head once with admiration and awe. "Of course we have to help them."

"Are we certain they won't make it?" the Doctor asked. "After all, we don't want to interfere if we don't have to."

"Good point, Doctor." Janeway put her hands firmly on the table. "We're reasonably certain, but we have to be absolutely certain. Seven, B'Elanna, I need those exact figures from you immediately."

"Aye, Captain," B'Elanna said.

"However, in the meantime," Janeway said, "we'll have to operate on the assumption that this ship will be destroyed in that explosion. I need suggestions, people, on how to save it."

"Hard to know where to begin," said Paris. "That thing is so big, its size alone limits our options. How do you help something almost two hundred kilometers long and tied together with basically bailing wire?"

"A tractor beam would shred it, even if it could

handle the weight and size," B'Elanna said. "This thing is so fragile that I'm afraid to touch it."

"Maybe we could find a way to boost their engines," Seven said.

"That might shred them too," B'Elanna said.

"Now you're beginning to understand our dilemma," Janeway said. "We don't have much time. I want some solutions, people, and I want them quickly. Is that understood?"

She was answered with nods all around.

She stood. "Meeting dismissed."

The staff pushed their chairs back and stood also. Janeway started out of the room, but Chakotay caught her arm.

"Kathryn," he said softly. "Are we even certain that these people will take our help?"

"At this moment, we're not sure of anything," she said, and let herself out of the room.

20 hours, 20 minutes

Emperor Aetayn remained rooted to his throne, ignoring the cacophony around him. His command center staff was giving orders, receiving information, and making certain that *Traveler* held together. They were doing their jobs.

And, in a strange way, he was doing his.

He was touring the devastation using his viewscreen. Many of the areas were blanked out. There was no reception at all. But from the areas on the fringe, he was getting a sense of the damage. And from what he could tell, "damage" was too small a word.

The asteroid had hit the unit about a third of the way from the front end. He assumed that the destruction anywhere near those holes was total. About halfway down the unit reception picked up and he could see fairly well. Homes had slid off their foundations, trees were down, buildings had been crumpled like sticks.

Farther on the damage seemed less and less.

But he wasn't looking at the actual physical damage as much as he was watching his people. They were pulling each other from the wreckage, tending each other's wounds, comforting each other in grief. They were taking heroic measures to save a small child from a collapsed building, pulling drowning people from a nearby river, using combined strength to pull vehicles—filled with families—out of what had become instant mud.

His people were going about the business of survival, even though he knew most of them only had a day to live.

Survival.

He clicked from image to image.

Survival everywhere he looked. The instinct was so strong in them. He rested his head on his chin, watching doctors perform triage in a makeshift medical center. So many clogged airholes (thank the skies for redundancy), so many fractured limbs, so many bleeding and near-death patients—all struggling to continue living one more day.

Somewhere in the last year, he had given up, succumbed to the inevitability of loss. As the statistics and hard data had come in, saying that *Traveler* had not gone far enough, that the explosion caused by the colliding suns would destroy her, he had nodded sagely and accepted the information.

Accepted it, as if they had no other choice.

He had doomed his people. He had gotten them this far, and he hadn't fought to get them farther. He had accepted the fatalism around him, overwhelmed by the task before him.

It had taken the disaster on Unit 3 to wake him up to the fact that he should be getting his hands dirty, pulling bleeding people from the wreckage, struggling to give them at least one more day of life.

He sat up and signaled impatiently with his right hand. Commander Gelet appeared at his side.

"Get me my car."

Gelet looked at the images playing on the viewscreen. "It's too soon to tour the devastation."

Touring the devastation. That was the job of a head of state, a man with little power and too much time on his hands. Aetayn was no longer going to be that man.

"I'm not going to Unit 3," he said. "I'm going to the Island."

"Beg pardon, Your Highness, but at this moment, the scientists cannot help Unit 3. They—"

"Get my car." Aetayn said sharply. "And send some of our top technicians to meet me there."

"Your Highness—"

"What part of my request do you not understand?"

Gelet straightened, but Aetayn saw the shock on his face. How long had he let his reign slip? How long had he let his unimaginative but capable commanders run this ship?

Too long? Was it too late?

He refused to believe that.

53

There had to be time to save *Traveler*. He would pull his people out before there was wreckage.

He had to.

There was no other choice.

20 hours, 10 minutes

Seven of Nine strode toward astrometrics. She had to recheck those figures for the captain, and then she had to figure out how to prevent future problems in her regeneration alcoves.

She would worry about that after she confirmed their current data on the stellar collision. Lieutenant Torres had returned to engineering to find the figures lost in the explosion. She had said she would meet Seven shortly in astrometrics.

Seven planned to have most of the work done by then. She could use Torres's help on the rebuilding of the alcove. Perhaps the two of them could discuss ways to save the alien ship while they were patching up the cargo bay.

She had just reached the the door to astrometrics when her combadge chirped.

"Seven of Nine, please report to the shuttlebay."

She did not recognize the voice, although it was vaguely familiar. Female and not the captain's. But right now the captain was busy with several things and it was not that unusual for her to delegate the task of contacting her crew members to someone else.

Seven tapped her combadge. "Acknowledged," she said.

She hoped that this diversion in the shuttlebay would not take too much of her time. She wanted to have those figures complete before Torres arrived in astrometrics.

She entered the turbolift. "Deck ten," she said.

The ride to the shuttlebay was short, but it seemed long. Seven felt the seconds ticking away. Whatever caused her summons had better be good.

She exited the turbolift and headed into the shuttlebay, leaving the corridor door open behind her. The lights were dim. The shuttles looked more like shadows than ships. She thought that odd. She took one more step inside, her footsteps echoing on the floor. It didn't feel like anyone else was in here. Now that was annoying. Had someone called her away from her duties on a whim?

Seven stopped beside the *Delta Flyer* and rapped on its side. No one answered. Not even Tom Paris was here, fiddling with his favorite toy. She was about to tap her combadge when the doors to the corridor slammed shut and chirruped as they did when they vacuum-locked.

Her breath caught. The corridor doors only locked like that when a shuttle was about to leave.

Sure enough, the bay doors rolled open and the air inside vented into space. The atmospheric forcefield that was ordinarily in place to prevent exactly such an occurrence was obviously inoperative.

Only her Borg-enhanced reflexes saved her from being blown into vacuum. Seven managed to grab on to the *Delta Flyer,* holding on with all her strength.

She had only a matter of seconds. Perhaps less if the craft wasn't massive enough to withstand the hurricane-force wind.

The *Delta Flyer* suddenly started to skid across the deck

Seven slammed her fist on the *Flyer*'s door. It opened.

She grabbed both sides of the doorframe and held herself in place. The force, pulling her toward the open bay doors, was incredible. It took all of her strength to hold herself in position. She wasn't sure she could throw herself inside the *Flyer*.

But she had to.

With all her strength, she flung herself inside, then wheeled around and manually closed the *Flyer*'s door, not willing to let any air out of her lungs.

The *Flyer*'s door closed.

The ship's environmental system automatically replenished the lost atmosphere. She took a deep breath. Air had never felt so good. She made her way to the cockpit and peered peered through its viewport into the bay.

The *Delta Flyer* had slid to halt just a few meters from the edge of the flight deck.

No shuttle exited. No shuttle entered.

"Computer," she said. "Who else is in the shuttlebay?"

"The shuttlebay is empty."

"What about the other shuttlecraft?"

"The other shuttlecraft are empty."

She sank into the *Flyer*'s command chair. *Not a malfunction.* She had been targeted deliberately. Again. Someone had lured her here and set the bay doors to open when she arrived. Luck and her quick thinking had saved her. Otherwise she would have been blown out into space, to die painfully.

Of all the deaths she knew of, dying unprotected in space was the one that she feared the most.

She would never confess that to anyone. She had only put it in her personal logs once and then erased it immediately. And she had never told a soul.

This was an attack of convenience, a startlingly easy attack at that. It would take little to set up, and even less effort to execute it.

She raised a shaking hand to her face, struggling for composure. *Not a malfunction.* The attack had been personal.

Someone on *Voyager* wanted her dead. One of her friends and colleagues had tried to kill her—twice.

Not a malfunction.

Chapter Three

"Captain," Kim said. "The shuttlebay doors just opened."

Janeway turned in her command chair. "Do we have an unauthorized shuttle launch in progress?" There was enough going on without another problem coming at her.

"No, Captain." Kim frowned at his console. "The atmospheric forcefield is offline. The bay is depressurized."

Chakotay had turned in his direction as well. "Close the doors and repressurize the bay."

"Aye, sir. . . . Captain? Someone's in there!"

"Oh?" Janeway asked. She felt tension tightening up her back. "Who?"

"Seven of Nine is in the *Delta Flyer,*" Kim said.

"She's supposed to be in astrometrics with

58

B'Elanna," Tom said. Janeway ignored him. She knew what Seven was supposed to be doing.

Janeway tapped her combadge. "Janeway to Seven of Nine. Seven, what's going on down there?"

There was no response. Janeway glanced at Kim. "Is she all right?"

Kim held out his hands in an I-don't-know gesture. "Her life signs read normal."

Janeway tapped her combadge again. "Seven, what are you doing in the *Delta Flyer?*"

"Captain," Seven said, "I would like to meet you in astrometrics. Alone."

Superficially, Seven's voice sounded as calm and strong as usual, but Janeway had become used to her nuances. Seven was shaken.

"What happened down there, Seven?"

"It would probably be wise to seal the shuttlebay to all personnel as soon as I leave," Seven said.

"Seven—"

"Please, Captain. This will be easier for both of us if we do it my way."

And with that Seven signed off. Janeway looked at Chakotay, who shrugged.

Janeway stood. Something very bad had just happened and she had no idea what it was. But her stomach was telling her it was worse than most anything.

"Perhaps one of us should accompany you," Tuvok said.

Janeway shook her head, suddenly remembering the explosion in the alcove. "Tuvok, did Seven order those doors to open?"

He tapped his console, then tilted his head slightly. "No, she did not."

"Who did?"

He worked for a moment longer. "I have no record of that command being issued."

Janeway frowned at him. "There should be a record."

"There should be," Tuvok agreed. "But I have none."

"Ensign Kim, do you?" Janeway asked.

Kim shook his head. "Nothing, Captain."

"Yet you're certain the doors opened."

"Yes, Captain." Kim stared at his console a moment longer. "And the system recorded my command to close the doors."

Janeway looked at Tuvok, who checked his own console and nodded. "Confirmed."

"Do we have a computer malfunction?" she asked. "Are some commands not making their way into the system?"

"It would take quite a while to check that," Kim said.

"You could run a diagnostic," Paris said.

"Assuming the computer can catch its own malfunctions."

"That is how it is designed, Ensign," Tuvok said. "I believe we should run the diagnostic and then evaluate the data, rather than anticipate it."

"Tuvok's right, Harry," Janeway said. "Let's see what the computer finds before we jump to conclusions. In the meantime, I'm heading to Astrometrics. You have the conn, Chakotay."

"Aye, Captain," he said, but she could hear the disapproval in his tone. He wasn't happy with the fact that she was going down there alone.

Did they suspect Seven of sabotaging the ship? Seven had proven her worth to *Voyager* over and over again. But strange things had happened in the last few hours, and Janeway wanted to get to the bottom of them.

19 hours, 36 minutes

The Island wasn't too far from the command center. Usually Emperor Aetayn walked to the shore of the small lake, where a private boat met him and ferried him across. This time, however, he took his aircar. His driver sped near the center of Unit 4 as he continued to watch the rescue efforts on his portable viewscreen.

More and more people were being pulled from the wreckage. The medical centers in Unit 3 were overflowing. He'd given the order to have some of the wounded transferred to Units 2 and 5.

It disturbed him that none of the surveillance equipment was working near the points of impact. If the damage was this severe at such a distance, it had to be devastating near the openings the asteroid had cut into the tube.

But until the rescue teams made it all the way inside, he would know nothing.

He hated knowing nothing.

Abruptly, the aircar landed on the Island. The landing was gentle, hardly disturbing his viewing, but he hadn't expected it. He had thought they were still some distance away, and hadn't even noticed the lake.

He turned off his viewer and stashed it in the pocket of his traveling suit. He had changed into his long golden waistcoat and matching trousers, the red tunic beneath worn to add formality. Even at times like these, clothing was important. Especially now, when his people were looking for order amid the chaos.

He stood, instructed his driver to remain, and exited the aircar. His security team followed, keeping a discreet distance. Other members of the team remained on the aircar to monitor everything from that location. He was also being monitored in the command center. His privacy had long ago been sacrificed to the greater good.

Two servants waited for him, bowing deeply when they saw him. Both were male, and the older one was balding, his skull turning a deep magenta where the hair used to be.

He walked past them, waving his fingers as he did so, indicating that they could stand. He knew the way to the compound. They didn't have to lead him there.

Instead, they followed, fifteen paces behind, just as they should have. He heard one of them radio ahead, letting the compound's staff know he had arrived.

The path led through a thicket. At this time of year, it was filled with climbing flowers, overgrown bushes, and thin grass. Later, it would be trimmed back and allowed to go dormant, simulating winter.

If there was going to be a later.

Then he stopped walking. Behind him, he heard a grunt as one of the servants stopped the other so that he remained the requisite fifteen paces back.

If there was going to be a later. It was precisely that kind of thinking that had gotten him into trouble. Precisely that which had led him to this moment now, when he could be surprised that his own people struggled to survive despite the odds against them.

He wasn't sure how he had become so complacent, but it had to stop, here and now.

He continued his walk through the thicket, down into the grove of trees that flanked the edge of the compound. The walkway twisted, then rose over a small hill.

The compound stretched before him, a dozen small buildings with windows on all sides. The U-shaped lab dominated the middle of the grounds. It had no windows at all and several guards at its doors. His subjects knew better than to approach the compound, but caution was the watchword here.

The guards bowed deeply as Aetayn passed. He did not acknowledge them. Instead, he stepped through the double doors and up the wooden steps. The conference area filled an entire section of this small building. It had been built so that the conference table was surrounded, on three sides, by massive windows, letting in the artificial light and the beauty of the gardens beyond. Since it was high summer in this tube, the windows were open, letting in the scents of pine, tuberoses, and mint.

His team of scientists were at the table, already kneeling. As he approached, all twenty of them bowed their heads in unison.

"Stand," he said. "We haven't time for this."

Then he turned to the servants and to his own security staff.

"Wait outside," he said.

That wasn't the normal protocol and one of his guards opened his mouth to say so. But Aetayn gave him a frosty glare and the guard seemed to think better of his objection. He bowed, then led the team outside.

Then Aetayn returned his attention to the scientists. They were standing near their chairs, studying him nervously.

He climbed the steps and took his place at the head of the table. As he sat, they did also. No one's head could be higher than the emperor's, a ruling he sometimes ignored, but most often took advantage of.

"Have you seen the devastation in Unit 3?" he asked.

They all faced him. They had a similarity of feature, probably caused by ten years in this place—their skin was an almost pinkish lavender, their eyes innocent but sharp. They wore their hair cropped short to keep it out of their faces. Their features differed, yet he had trouble seeing them as individuals. He never met with them alone. They were, to him, a twenty-person organism that he interacted with on an occasional basis.

Right now, their joint expression was one of surprise. They hadn't expected him to ask that question.

Reflet, the most senior scientist, a man who always sat to Aetayn's right, said, "We had heard of the accident, but we've been working."

Accident. Did they always speak in euphemisms? Had he caught that habit as well, learning the words that minimized an event rather than accurately described it?

"I hope you've been double-checking your calculations," he said.

They nodded as a group. It was uncanny, really,

the way they seemed to move together. It unnerved him every time he came here.

"The suns will collide in less than a Rhawnian day," Reflet said, enmphasizing the "Rhawnian." Originally he had objected to using the Rhawnian units of measure, saying that they now needed a universal way to measure time, but Aetayn had resisted. It had been one of the few times he had stood up to these people.

He squared his shoulders, uncertain why his scientists intimidated him.

"The collision will result in an explosion that will have a wide radius of effect. Unfortunately, we are not clear of the blast radius. Not long after the collision takes place, *Traveler* will be vaporized."

A shudder ran down his back. *Unfortunately.* So sad. It'll be over soon and that's regrettable. Aetayn bit the side of his cheek, feeling the pain before he spoke.

"What are your solutions?" he asked.

The scientists looked at each other. He had asked this question before, and then the answer had been that there was no solution.

"Your Excellency," Reflet said. "We have done the best we can. Unfortunately our ship was designed before our expertise allowed us to accurately estimate the trajectory of the suns. We have done our best—"

"What," Aetayn said slowly and clearly, "are your solutions?"

The scientists looked at each other again.

"There are none," Reflet said.

Aetayn glared at them, feeling his own father in his gaze. His father would never have allowed this. His father was the one who had gotten *Traveler* built. His father would have been appalled that these scientists had given up. His father would have made them find a solution.

But his father had given up, if his journals were to be believed. He had accepted the error and then died, leaving Aetayn to rule over a doomed people.

"Do you all believe there are no solutions?"

His voice didn't even sound like his own. It had an imperious ring to it. His life had been too soft. He hadn't been challenged. He had not been faced with anything difficult, until now.

And he had denied that until it was probably too late.

A woman at the other end of the table raised her hand. It wobbled in the air, shaking as if with nerves. Reflet glared at her, made a quick gesture with his own hand, as if her action embarrassed him. She brought her hand down.

"No," Aetayn said. "I'd like to hear what she has to say."

He nodded at her. She flushed violet, and then closed her eyes, as if gathering herself. Her hair was slightly longer than the others', her clothing rumpled. She almost looked as if she didn't belong.

Why hadn't he noticed her before?

Because she hid well. She hadn't wanted to be noticed, even now.

She opened her eyes. He saw deep intelligence in them warring with uncertainty.

"I've been speaking to some of the technicians," she said, and he started. The technicians were going to be his next meeting. "They believe they can tweak the engines and the thrusters to increase our speed by at least one percent."

"That won't be enough." Reflet spoke with contempt.

"I did not give you leave to enter this discussion," Aetayn snapped. "Pray continue——?"

He paused, waiting for her name.

Her flush grew. "Detia."

"Detia." A pretty name for a pretty woman. His sadness grew. There was so much he had missed here, so much he had let slip by him. "Please continue."

"I believe that if we can increase by one percent, we might be able to increase by more. We might have a chance to outrun this thing. . . ." Her voice trailed off. Reflet was staring at her, clearly intimidating her.

"You're dismissed," Aetayn said to him.

"Your Excellency," Reflet began.

"Dare you continue to contradict me?" Truly the voice that came out of him was no longer his own. It had been possessed by his father and grandfather.

Reflet bowed his head. "No, Excellency."

"Then you are dismissed."

Reflet stood, then realized he had forgotten the necessary bow. He knelt, and lowered his head. Aetayn let him stay in that position for a long, long moment. Reflet squirmed.

Finally, Aetayn waved his hand in dismissal. Reflet hurried from the room.

"One percent is very small," Aetayn said to Detia.

She nodded. "Our calculations weren't off by much. Every advantage we can get will be helpful, even at this late date. Temblet and Petla have been experimenting with a forcefield——"

"Detia," someone said softly, reprimanding her.

"——but it hasn't come to anything yet." She leaned

67

forward, caught up in her own words now. "But if there's anything I've learned about science, Excellency, it's that breakthroughs can happen in less than a day."

His breath caught. This was why his people were pulling each other from rubble. This was why they had built *Traveler,* this unguarded optimism, the hope he had closed his heart to over the past few weeks.

"Explain this forcefield to me," he said toward the table, uncertain who Temblet and Petla were.

A thin man near Detia shot her a nervous glance, then said, "We had the idea that we could build an energy wall that would deflect the worst of the explosion away from us. The problem is that field would take a great deal of energy, more than we know how to generate. And we would have no way to test this. If we gambled on it, and we failed—"

"Then we at least tried," Aetayn said.

"Our resources are limited, Excellency," said the woman beside the man. She was clearly Petla. "If we use the energy to build our forcefield, then we cannot use it to propel the ship farther forward."

"It's in our best interest to get as far from those suns as possible," said another scientist.

Aetayn agreed with that, but the beginnings of a plan were forming in his mind. "Do we have other options?"

"These are not options, Excellency," said the scientist to his immediate left. "These are fantasies."

Ah, one of Reflet's companions in passivity. Aetayn turned toward him. "What would you suggest we do?"

"Tell our people so that they might prepare themselves for the inevitable."

Aetayn thought of the medical teams, triaging, making judgments about who had the best chance of survival. Those were not people who would prepare for the inevitable. Those were people who believed in fighting until the death.

So did he. He was stunned to realize that was how he felt. He had buried it so deeply that he hadn't recognized the emotion until now.

"Would *Traveler* have any more of a chance if we evacuated one-tenth of the population?" he asked.

The nineteen remaining scientists stared at him again. He was beginning to get used to their collective shock.

"Evacuated to where?" one of them asked.

"Deep space," Aetayn said.

"How would you propose to do that?" Temblet asked.

"We have smaller ships, hundreds of them," Aetayn said, "the ones that brought us to *Traveler* as well as the emergency ships. If we filled them and sent them to a coordinate in deep space, out of the danger area, and had them wait for us, would those people have a chance of surviving? And also, would it help *Traveler*?"

The word "us" startled him as much as it seemed to startle them. Detia pulled on her lower lip.

"Lessening the weight would not help," Detia said. "The mass of *Traveler* is so big that I doubt . . ." She paused, as if she was considering. "We'll have to do the math."

"We could get rid of nonessential items as well," Aetayn said. "We would jettison them."

"Nonessential items?" asked the scientist next to

him. "There are no such things. When we boarded this ship we were to bring only the most important items in our lives, nothing more. I don't see how we could winnow that down any further."

Aetayn frowned at him. "It's a choice between dying and surviving. Losing your possessions, it seems to me, is a small price to pay for living."

No one spoke. He nodded into the silence.

"Do your calculations. I want to know whether a lighter load will speed *Traveler* up enough to make a difference. And if not, would the people we send ahead, out of danger, have any chance of survival? I need that information within the hour."

"We'll do it, Excellency," Detia said. Apparently his attention to her had put her in charge of the group. That relieved him. She seemed to share his sensibilities, unlike Reflet.

Aetayn stood and all of the scientists fell to their knees, showing him respect. He wanted to wave it away, but he did not. Instead he headed down the steps, feeling a small shred of hope.

Even if *Traveler* did not survive, a few of his people might. The smaller ships weren't built for deep space, but they had a chance. If they equipped them properly and put the right people in them, the chances might be pretty good that his race would not die.

He'd have to figure out who went on those ships. This time, it would be his decision. He would not take his father's route—that whoever could afford passage would be the one allowed to go. That choice of his father's had bothered Aetayn from the beginning and had led, he believed, to a poor representation of Rhawn on *Traveler.*

Not that it mattered anymore. Those too poor to board *Traveler* were dead now. But he wondered how hard they would have fought to stay alive, and when they would have started that fight. He doubted they would have just accepted their fate.

A shiver ran through him as he understood the implications of his thought. Even though they had been denied passage on *Traveler*, they probably had fought to survive.

But they had failed.

Will alone wouldn't do this. They needed something more.

He just hoped that he would find it in time.

18 hours, 50 minutes

This time, Janeway held the meeting in her ready room. She didn't want the entire senior staff there. She only wanted the ones she could trust. She brought in Seven, because incidents were happening to her, as well as Tuvok, Janeway's oldest and dearest friend, and Chakotay, who had become her right arm.

While she talked with them, she held a cup of black coffee. It warmed her hands, which had grown inexplicably cold.

She had gone to astrometrics to see Seven and found the normally collected woman to be shaking and pale. Seven had tried to act as if she were all right, but Janeway knew that she was deeply upset.

As Seven related her the story, Janeway realized that Seven had survived thanks to a combination of luck, intuition, and intelligence. Twice now, events had conspired to save Seven's life.

71

Janeway did not want there to be a need for a third time. And given the unusual nature of the "incident," she didn't doubt Seven's assertion that they were no accidents.

But first she had to solve three questions. Who was targeting Seven? Why Seven? And why now? She was a member of this crew, and had come a long way since her ties to the Borg collective had first been severed, a time when Seven had been volatile and unpredictable, unable to shed her Borg mindset.

Except for the few, always tragic casualties they'd endured over the years since, the same crew was on *Voyager* now as then, but now it appeared that one of them wanted Seven dead.

Unless there was someone new aboard. It wasn't unprecedented for an alien presence to act undetected aboard *Voyager*, and it wasn't a possibility she was going to ignore.

Janeway stared at the stars while Seven completed her story for a second time, informing Chakotay and Tuvok of all that had happened. This time, Seven's voice didn't shake. This time, Seven seemed calm.

Although Janeway thought she heard a hint of anger beneath that oh-so-placid surface.

"I have been monitoring the entire ship since the first incident," Tuvok said. "There are no obvious signs of an intruder."

"Besides the attack on Seven, you mean," Chakotay said.

"We cannot assume that an intruder attacked her," Tuvok said. "The evidence is far from conclusive."

Janeway turned. Seven was staring at the windows, just as Janeway had been. Her expression was even, although her lower lip trembled, ever so slightly.

"Whoever did this to me," Seven said without looking at the two men, "knew me and knew my routine. I would have been in the deepest part of my regenerative cycle when the alcove exploded. This time, I was called by name and asked to go to the shuttlebay."

"Seven," Janeway said gently, "you don't always do what I tell you. Why did you follow this particular command?"

Seven's large eyes met Janeway's. It seemed clear that Seven was asking herself the same question.

"The message was that I was to report to the shuttlebay. I believed that you were too busy to give the order yourself, so I assumed you had asked someone else to do it."

"Did this mysterious person use my name?"

Seven shook her head.

"Yet you thought the command came from me."

Seven shrugged one elegant shoulder. "When you are in command, Captain, no one else tells me what to do."

Janeway suppressed a smile. No one else dared. Or rarely, anyway. Besides, Seven had made it clear from the beginning that she preferred to take her orders from the captain—and even those she rarely followed to the letter.

"Yet whoever planned this seemed to know that you would follow this order," Janeway said.

"We cannot assume that, Captain," Tuvok said.

"Do you believe this was a random attack?" Chakotay asked. "That whoever did this would have been satisfied no matter who walked into the shuttlebay?"

"That is not what I am saying." Tuvok gestured toward the replica of *Voyager* on a nearby table. "While the methodology of the attack may seem crude, it is not. It shares an element of subtlety with the previous incident, one that is not readily apparent."

Janeway hadn't seen this attack as subtle, and was interested to hear why her chief of security thought it was. "Go on, Tuvok."

"Just as the timing in the first attack was set to coincide with the moment when Seven was most vulnerable—"

Seven winced at that characterization. Tuvok did not seem to notice.

"—this new attack was also devised to catch her at an unaware moment."

"I knew something was wrong when I entered the shuttlebay," Seven said.

"Yes," Tuvok said. "And that awareness in all likelihood saved your life. But I am not referring to that in particular. I am referring to the way in which this attack was structured."

"If I had walked into that shuttlebay at the wrong moment, I would have probably been blown into space," Chakotay said.

"Unlikely," Tuvok said. "I believe this attack was structured so that the bay doors would open only when Seven entered the shuttlebay."

"Do you have evidence of this, Tuvok?" Janeway asked.

"Not yet," Tuvok said. "But it is logical. The doors did not open until she was inside and yet she was alone. Somehow the perpetrator had to have known the precise moment when Seven entered the shuttlebay. He could not have calculated—"

"She," Seven said.

Janeway looked at her.

Seven shrugged again. "The voice was female. I had forgotten that until now."

Tuvok nodded, as if he were taking in the information. "*She* could not have calculated the time it would take for Seven to travel from astrometrics to the shuttlebay. Someone could have stopped Seven or she could have chosen not to go at all. Yet the doors opened after the corridor doors had shut—the only way for this attack to work, and to contain its effects."

"You think she was being watched?" Chakotay asked.

"Or monitored," Janeway said, thinking of the various ways that could be done.

"No," Tuvok said. "I suspect the shuttlebay doors were set to open the moment a sensor notified the system of Seven's presence."

"Through her combadge?" Janeway asked, feeling appalled that the communications system could be used like that.

"Perhaps. Or, possibly, through her Borg implants. While someone else on the ship could conceivably carry Seven's combadge into the shuttlebay, no one else could have those implants."

Seven shuddered. The movement was faint, but Janeway caught it out of the corner of her eye.

"What you're suggesting requires a great deal of sophistication," Janeway said.

"The first attack also took sophistication," Tuvok

said. "After all, we have no record of tampering before the attack occurred."

"So now you're calling it an attack." Seven's voice was harsh. Janeway sighed. The anger Seven had been suppressing was coming out sideways, as it often did. But Janeway did not step in. Tuvok could defend himself.

"The circumstances of the second incident have caused me to reexamine my assumptions about the first," Tuvok said.

"Before you thought I might have tampered with my own alcove."

"I never made such an accusation."

"No," Seven said. "You implied it."

Tuvok straightened, as he often did when he was feeling insulted. Janeway remained very still, waiting.

"I was evaluating all possibilities," Tuvok explained. "I never believed you deliberately sabotaged your own alcove. However, the thought did occur to me that your constant work on the alcove could have set up some sort of systems failure."

"Making the explosion my fault."

"I am not assigning blame—"

"No one is." Janeway finally stepped in. The tension level was high enough. "We now know that someone has targeted Seven. We need to know who has done this and why."

"And we need to know it quickly," Chakotay said. "Whether it's an intruder, or someone in the crew, the situation presents a danger to the entire ship, not just Seven. And there's still the matter of that alien ship. If we're going to do anything for it, we may have to channel all our resources toward it soon. Millions of lives are at stake."

Seven bristled. Janeway could sense her misunderstanding of the comment. Janeway held up her hand.

"Tuvok, I want you to make these attacks on Seven your highest priority. If you need assistance, come to any of us in this room."

Chakotay seemed surprised. "What about the rest of the senior staff?"

"I don't want any more distractions," Janeway lied. The truth was, she wasn't sure who she could trust. Tuvok's points about the attacks' sophistication made her wonder even more about who had initiated it. Whoever it was had to have a lot of technical expertise, suggesting a lot of experience in areas that most of *Voyager*'s crew did not have.

Seven was watching her closely.

"What we've discussed goes no farther than this room," Janeway said. "I don't want anyone else on the ship to know the severity of this second attack."

"Shouldn't we give Seven some protection?" Chakotay asked. "Maybe a guard?"

"If someone had been with me in the shuttlebay, he would not have survived." Seven spoke with her normal unconscious arrogance. But she was right. No one else would have survived that.

"I think the best way to protect Seven," Tuvok said, "is to find the mind behind these attacks as quickly as possible."

"I don't want you to work on anything else," Janeway said. "Give this your full attention, Tuvok."

"Aye, Captain."

"Now," Janeway said. "We need to turn our attention to that alien ship. On this matter, I can use the full senior staff. Let's reconvene on the bridge."

Tuvok and Chakotay led the way out the door. As they left, Janeway caught Seven's arm.

"Will you be all right?"

"I have survived worse, Captain," Seven said.

"Yes, you have," Janeway said, "but if you're going to help with this alien ship, I need you at the top of your game."

"I have already reworked the calculations," Seven said. "I shall be fine."

Janeway studied her for a moment.

Seven tilted her head slightly. "I prefer working, Captain, to worrying. I will be able to give this matter my fullest concentration."

"That's all I needed to hear," Janeway said and led the way to the bridge. She tapped her combadge as she walked. "B'Elanna, please join us on the bridge."

"Acknowledged," B'Elanna said through the badge, her voice sounding small. The combadge did distort the voice slightly, but it was still recognizable. Janeway frowned, wondering if Seven would be able to listen to all the female voices on the ship filtered through a combadge and isolate the one voice that had summoned her to the shuttlebay.

It was an idea to follow up on if Tuvok found nothing.

Janeway walked to her command chair and studied her bridge crew. Chakotay sat beside her and Tuvok went to his position at security, probably to check the computer logs. Harry Kim stood at his station, working diligently as always. Tom Paris was at the helm and Ensign Messingham worked beside him. Other members of the crew went about their duties as if nothing were wrong.

Perhaps for them, nothing was.

But everything seemed distorted to Janeway. She felt as if someone had blown a hole in her world. She found herself hoping that there was an intruder on board. It would be easier to handle than having one of her own crew members using the ship as a weapon against another crew member.

Seven stood beside Janeway, hands clasped behind her back, studying the bridge as if she had never seen it before. If Janeway felt this disconcerted, she could imagine how Seven felt. Twice attacked, both times narrowly escaping with her life. When she had come on board, Janeway had promised her she would always be safe here, that *Voyager* was her home. It had taken almost two years of struggle, but Seven had finally accepted her place on *Voyager.*

And now this.

"All right, Mr. Kim. Put the alien ship on screen," Janeway said.

The ship appeared, vast and unwieldy. Smaller craft seemed to be working around the damaged area.

"Do you think they know that they aren't going to make it?" Paris asked as he watched.

"They sure aren't acting that way," Ensign Messingham said.

"What, you think they should just give in?" Paris said. "Not repair the ship and see what happens?"

She shrugged. "I would evacuate the damaged section and then jettison it."

"That ship doesn't have the capability to jettison a damaged section," Kim said. "It functions as one piece. One badly put together piece, but one piece just the same. One broken link, and it's all over."

"I do not believe it to be badly put together," Tuvok said from his post behind Janeway. "Considering the technology disadvantages this species has, the ship before us is very well constructed."

"A miracle ship."

That voice was new. Janeway turned. Neelix had joined them. She had been concentrating so hard on the ship that she hadn't heard the turbolift open.

He nodded toward her and then came forward. He was holding a steel thermos. "I made you some special coffee. It's a *mocha*. I have been reading about Earth coffee drinks and this one sounded especially suited to you."

She wanted to ask him what prompted this generosity, why he was buttering her up now, but she didn't. Neelix was often generous for no apparent reason, with no desire for gain from that generosity. She mentally shook herself. This suspicion would get her nowhere and only hurt her command.

"Thank you, Mr. Neelix," she said taking the silver cup he offered her. The smell was warm and delicious, a mixture of hot cocoa and coffee. If nothing else, the caffeine would jolt her system for hours to come.

"Is that the ship I've heard so much about?" Neelix asked, and then she understood why he was here. She hadn't included him in the recent meetings, although she often considered him part of her senior staff. He'd obviously decided to get involved in his own way.

"Yeah," Paris said. "What do you think?"

"It has an awkward beauty," Neelix said. "Rather like that look children get as they go into their first teenage growth spurt."

Janeway glanced at him. The description was curiously apt. A species that first ventured into space was like a child hitting puberty. It had no idea about the adventure before it, but it was willing to give that adventure a chance.

The turbolift swished open and B'Elanna stepped on deck. "Sorry," she said rather breathlessly. "I wanted to double-check the figures one last time."

Seven glared at her. "We went over the figures more than two dozen times."

"Yes," B'Elanna said. She made her way down the stairs so that she stood near Tom Paris. "But we're talking about stepping into another culture's future. We had to make absolutely sure. If we could avoid this, we should."

"Our figures were correct." That anger of Seven's was leaking out sideways again.

"What's your conclusion?" Janeway asked, wanting to ease the tension between the two women.

Seven raised an eyebrow at B'Elanna as if to say, *You were the one who had to check the figures one last time. You tell her.*

"In a little less than nineteen hours," B'Elanna said, "those suns will collide, creating an explosion that will reach the alien ship."

"But they can ride the wave, right?" Neelix sounded hopeful. He hadn't been part of the earlier meetings. He had no idea how grave this was.

"There is no wave to ride," Seven said. "The force

81

caused by the matter spraying outward will vaporize that ship."

"What about deflector shields?" Neelix asked. "Surely they would protect it."

"Their technology is too primitive," Seven said. "We do not believe they have shields."

"If they had any," Kim said, "they wouldn't have been hit by that asteroid."

"Oh." Neelix nodded sagely. "Unless they hadn't known it was coming."

"Which suggests their technology is even poorer than we thought," Seven said. "Before they got into space, they should have had the ability to monitor what is going on outside their hull."

Janeway had had enough chatter. "We're acting on supposition now," she said. "We need facts. The facts are that this is a primitive ship filled with eight hundred million beings and that it's defenseless against the coming explosion. I'm not prepared to sit idly by while these people are incinerated. Ideas?"

"Most of the things I've come up with aren't functional for a ship of that size," Kim said, as if he could sense Janeway's growing frustration.

"I suppose there are no hospitable planets that we could evacuate them to and help them settle on?" Neelix asked.

"None close enough to save even a small fraction of the population," Kim said.

"I've come up with a long shot," Torres said. "We might be able to tie *Voyager* to the alien ship's superstructure and use impulse drive to shove it out of harm's way."

"Push the ship like a car stuck in the mud?" Paris asked.

The analogy made sense only to the history buffs on the crew. Janeway was one of them and she gave Paris half a smile.

"We'd apply our own thrust to give it the momentum it needed to get out of the way," Torres said. "It wouldn't have to be much. Just enough to help them clear the danger zone in time."

"Well, that's a positive recommendation," Paris said, but his tone was teasing. Torres smiled at him.

"Your suggestion is flawed," Seven said.

Torres's smile left her face. The entire bridge crew looked at Seven. Janeway leaned back in her command chair, waiting for Seven's explanation.

"The alien ship cannot take the stress your idea would force upon it," Seven said. "Such an attempt would tear the ship apart."

"I admit that it's a risk," Torres said. "But as far as I can tell, it's their only chance."

"How much of a risk is it?" Janeway asked.

Torres shrugged. "Without making a closer study of that ship, I don't know for certain. They're using some alloys that are unfamiliar to me. Their superstructure that is holding all those tubes together might be tougher than we think it is."

"It might also be weaker," Paris said.

Torres shot him a look that was withering. She had clearly expected more support from him. Paris caught that too. He shrugged and turned his palms upward in a gesture of surrender.

"I was not referring to the hull," Seven said. "I was referring to the magnetic juncture points. They are quite fragile. Your plan would increase the torque. The juncture points will not withstand the stress."

"Sometimes," Neelix said, "something that looks fragile can be quite strong."

Bravo, Mr. Neelix, Janeway thought. "Well," she said, "until someone comes up with something better, this is our plan."

"Captain," Seven said, "I must object."

"Your objection is noted, Seven." Janeway turned slightly in her chair so that she wouldn't be facing Seven. "Ensign Paris, bring us in closer to that alien ship. Ensign Kim, hail them."

"Let's hope they really have thought about the possibility of alien life forms," Kim mumbled. "Otherwise this is going to be quite a shock."

"It's probably going to be quite a shock anyway," Janeway said. Making first contact—real first contact, not a hidden one—with a prewarp culture was not in the instruction manual. The key was to do it simply, and with a minimum of fuss.

And hope that the aliens responded in kind.

Chapter Four

18 hours, 31 minutes

Lyspa hovered over her daughter, ignoring the cries and moans around her. People had begun to move the overturned carts, push aside the fallen trees, and dig beneath the fallen structures to find victims. Others had started to work on the entrance to the viewpark, hoping that they'd find a way out and back home.

Cyot had taken a small knife from his pocket and had seared it over some of the still hot controls of one of the carts. The metal had turned an angry red. He'd let it cool before he went to work on Andra.

The knife made Lyspa nervous. She wondered if Cyot had lied to her, if, indeed, he was some sort of intern. He had acted like one, but it wasn't common for anyone of good standing to carry weapons in the viewpark.

Emperor Aetayn had said that all of the bad elements of Rhawn society had not been allowed on *Traveler*, but the last ten years had proven that wrong. They'd had to set up jails in each of the units and the council had even voted on whether or not criminals—no matter what the crime—had the right to live on *Traveler*. So far, the ruling had been that the laws of Rhawn applied: criminals deserved imprisonment and rehabilitation, not death. But their prison population was still small. Experts were predicting that if the population grew, the death-penalty issue would come up again and again.

Lyspa shook her head. Amazing the things that were going through her mind. She wondered if she was more badly injured than she had thought. She certainly couldn't seem to concentrate on anything.

Except Andra and those junction doors.

Andra made two sharp moans of pain. Two lines of pale purple blood ran down her neck like celebratory bands.

"Oh, Mother," she said, her precious voice back. It sounded bubbly, as if there were blood in her throat. But at least she could talk.

Cyot crouched near her, examining her face, then her arms, and finally her legs. Lyspa watched him. The knife had returned to his pocket and he no longer seemed as threatening. His long fingers were gentle on her daughter's skin. Lyspa wondered how she had doubted him.

"She's going to need help," he said to Lyspa. "And soon."

Lyspa turned toward the entrance. It was still blocked. A handful of people were removing the rubble, one piece at a time. The longer she looked at it, the more she realized that the rubble had come from outside the door, not from the viewpark itself.

This was getting worse and worse.

She glanced in the other direction at the tilted signs.

DO NOT ENTER
JUNCTURE POINT
AUTHORIZED PERSONNEL ONLY

"How soon?" Lyspa asked, still staring at the signs.

He didn't answer. She looked at him. His eyes were eloquent and they told her that he didn't want to speak in front of her daughter. They told her that unless they got Andra out of here, she'd lose the use of her legs.

Or she'd die.

"We're not going to get through that door," Lyspa said.

"You're not thinking of going to Unit 4, are you?"

It was Lyspa's turn not to answer.

"You know that contact between the units is forbidden without express permission."

"I think an emergency is express permission," Lyspa said.

"No, Mother," Andra said. "We can wait."

But they couldn't wait, that was the thing. They had to get her out of here.

"How many others are going to need immediate medical treatment?" Lyspa asked.

Cyot looked around. His expression grew sad. Lyspa made herself look as well, not at the physical damage, but at the people.

Some were laid out on the floor, as Andra was,

and many were not moving. They had been placed side by side, leading Lyspa to believe they were dead. Others were lying nearer to the main door, twisting and moaning.

One woman, who was on her back, held her face and rocked from side to side. A man cradled his arm, which bent unnaturally away from him. Several children sat together, watching everything with wide eyes.

The children unnerved Lyspa the most. They seemed to be so overwhelmed by the situation that they couldn't even cry, and no one seemed to be taking care of them.

Maybe there was no one left who could.

Lyspa realized then that Cyot was saying nothing. His gaze met hers, that eloquent gaze, and in it, she saw confirmation of all that she already knew.

"The able-bodied should be getting people from the wreckage," he said softly.

"Yes," she said, "but who is going to go through that door for help?"

He was silent for a moment longer; then he said, "What if that section is damaged too? We have no idea what happened here. For all we know, the juncture could have split off. Maybe that's why no one from that section has come to help us."

Lyspa shook her head. "We're too stable for that. If our junction had broken, we'd still be suffering the effects of it, and the emergency ships wouldn't be focusing on this unit. They'd be focusing on the junction."

"If they're all right," Andra said, her voice still bubbling, "then why haven't they come to help us?"

Lyspa ran a hand over her daughter's hair. "They

need permission, Andra. And Emperor Aetayn hasn't given it to them."

Aetayn sat in his throne because his legs could not hold him. He stared at his viewscreen, at the sleek, elegant, *foreign* vessel that headed toward *Traveler.*

He had been in his aircar, heading back from the Island, when one of his assistants told him that an alien craft was approaching. The words "alien craft" had startled him. The possibility of meeting alien beings in space had been theorized since long before *Traveler*'s launch, but no one had really expected they would ever encounter such beings.

He instructed his driver to hurry back to the command center. The car had taken him to his own entrance, and he had hurried inside, glancing at the larger viewscreens and seeing the ship, long and clean and perfect, with no visible seams or rotating parts.

It was bigger than any of the other ships the Rhawns had built to serve *Traveler.* And it had a grace that his engineers could only aspire to. It moved with speed that had been unimaginable to his people, speed that he envied.

If *Traveler* had that kind of speed, it wouldn't be in danger now.

His people had once imagined that beings— gods—lived in the skies. Many had clung to that belief, long after Rhawns had conquered the air. A few still clung to that belief after Rhawns had entered space.

The true believers had refused to leave Rhawn,

saying that the Sky Singers would protect them and their planet from destruction. They had not, of course. Those Rhawns were dead.

But the old myths were powerful, and seeing a craft come from the darkness brought to mind all of those childhood stories, all of those ancient beliefs.

A god, coming from the sky, to save them in their hour of need.

"Do you think they're peaceful?" Erese was asking Gelet.

The question brought Aetayn out of his reverie. The screen made things look unreal. Even the destruction, while it had been horrible, hadn't been entirely real to him.

"Sir," one of the crew said to the ship's commander, Iquagt. "They're hailing us."

"How do you know it's a hail?" Iquagt asked, his head bent over his console.

Aetayn tore his gaze away from the viewscreen. Good question. How did they know?

"Um, because, sir, they're doing it in our own language."

A hush fell over the command center.

No one moved.

Maybe the others felt as he did, that the myth of the Sky Singers had come too closely to life.

Only Iquagt seemed unmoved. "Your Excellency," he said, "I believe this falls under your jurisdiction, not mine."

For a moment, Aetayn froze. Ship-to-ship communication was traditionally the job of the ship's commander.

But diplomacy was the job of the emperor.

Diplomacy.

He swallowed, hoping that his momentary confusion hadn't shown on his face.

"Answer their hail," he said in a tone that implied that such communication was the most normal thing in the world.

Instantly, the scene of the viewscreens changed. A woman stood before them, a recognizable woman with skin an unnatural shade of yellow. Beside her was a man who had something dark drawn onto his face, and more strangely colored people. Some had brown skin, others that funny yellow. Their hair was brown or yellow or black, not any of the beautiful colors his people favored.

In fact there was no purple anywhere that he could see. The view seemed strange to him partly because it was that the aliens weren't alien enough. They seemed like creatures in a dream, unnatural but not unimaginable.

"Greetings." The woman did speak his language.

His hands were clammy. He clasped them in his lap. His mouth was dry and he wondered if he should speak too.

"I'm Captain Kathryn Janeway of the Federation starship *Voyager*. We see that you are in trouble. We hope that we might be of assistance."

Aetayn shook that eerie feeling of myth coming to life. The words, even though they were in his language, seemed strange to him. Starship? Federation? Captains? What was all of this?

"I am Emperor Aetayn, leader of the Rhawnian people." He hesitated just briefly. He didn't dare tell them that this ship held his entire civilization. What if these aliens were only playing at kindness? He didn't want to give them more information than necessary. "I have never heard of your Federation."

The purposeful petulance in his tone sounded almost ungrateful, but he knew that was how his father would have conducted this discussion. Maintain the upper hand in all situations. Make certain that they catered to you instead of you giving in to them.

To his surprise, the alien woman smiled. "The United Federation of Planets exists on the other side of the galaxy, in a different quadrant. I guess you could say we are the ambassadors to this quadrant."

Now he was getting even more confused.

"The Federation is an interstellar alliance of planetary governments," she said. "We have more than a hundred and fifty member worlds across eight thousand light-years. We are a peaceful organization, dedicated to trade and exploration, among other things. *Voyager* is primarily a scientific vessel. We came your way to study the collision of the two stars. We hadn't expected to find another vessel here."

A vessel. As if *Traveler* were simply a ship that crossed deep space, and not the hope of his people.

He tried to wrap his mind around everything she had told him. Alliance? Planetary governments, over a hundred and fifty of them? There were that many aliens in the universe, enough to form an alliance? Against other aliens?

She was watching him as if his confusion were something she understood. It amazed him that she could see him. Obviously the system they had placed in *Traveler* to communicate with Rhawn as the exodus was taking place still worked. But that it worked across space and with different technology startled him.

Everything about this meeting startled him, the aliens most of all. They were so casual about their appearance. They had been studying the suns, as if the suns were a curiosity instead of the end of everything he knew.

"I see I have surprised you," she said after a moment.

His father would have been disappointed in him. He had lost the advantage. Maybe he had lost the advantage when the alien ship appeared. Try as he might, Aetayn could not remain casual about this.

"You are the first alien life we've encountered," he said, dropping the petulant tone. "To say that there are over a hundred and fifty others requires me to make a mental shift that is . . ."

Words failed him. He had to shake his head.

She studied him with what seemed like great compassion. "The stars are full of life and civilizations. Many of those lives look a lot like us. Others are so foreign that it's almost impossible to understand them. Yet we try."

They try.

"You study them like you study our suns?"

"Sometimes," she said, but she didn't elaborate. There seemed to be an entire world of stories implied in that one word.

"You think you can help us?" He tried to sound casual, but he could hear the need in his voice.

"We're not sure," she said.

He felt his heart sink, and he resisted the urge to rub the pressure points on the side of his nose. No need to let these marvelous creatures know how upset he was.

"We are working on some possible solutions," she was saying. "If we find one, we are more than willing to try."

Try. That made them different from the sky creatures of myth. Those creatures would have had a solution, and they would have known it would work.

"For all your effort, what will we owe you?" he asked, fearful of the response.

She smiled at him. "Nothing but friendship. We are passing through this area on a long journey. We just hope we can help."

Aetayn's skin went cold. The price was hidden then. He would accept their help and then find out the cost later.

But the cost really didn't matter. Either his people survived or they didn't. If they did survive, he was willing to pay whatever price these strange aliens exacted. Any price would be worthwhile for the people of Rhawn to have a future.

18 hours, 8 minutes

Lyspa helped Cyot right another cart. Then she turned away, her stomach churning.

The woman beneath the cart was dead. Her chest had been crushed. Bones pierced the skin, leaving the entire area a bloody mass.

Andra lay with the other wounded, talking with them, helping as best she could. She had mobility in her upper torso, which was more than most of them had, but her energy was failing. Lyspa could see it.

"I can't do this anymore."

She couldn't believe the words had left her mouth.

Cyot wiped his hands on his pants. "What?"

"I can't. If I rescue people, I'm only prolonging the inevitable." Lyspa turned toward him. "I'm going to take Andra through that door. You can follow me, if you like."

He stared at her. "You could lose everything."

Lyspa looked at her daughter, talking to the person next to her. The expression on Andra's face was one of calm concern. Even though her daughter was gravely injured, she still found the ability to help someone else.

"No," Lyspa said. "If I stay here, I'll lose everything."

He made no response. This time, she took his silence for confirmation. Or at least acquiescence.

"You won't be able to carry her that far," he said finally.

"Sure I will." Lyspa had a wiry strength and she knew that determination counted for as much as her muscle mass. If it meant saving Andra's life, then Lyspa could carry her for days.

"No," he said. "I meant, I can help."

She turned toward him, tempted—more than tempted—to take his offer. It would make her life much easier.

But she couldn't.

"You're needed here," she said. "You have medical training. Most people don't. Get people out."

"While you go to safety."

She shook her head. "I have a reason to try the juncture. You don't. If they grant me leniency, they'll do it because of Andra's injuries. You'll have no such excuse."

She wasn't used to being this selfless. He glanced at the wreckage, at the other people still digging through the rubble. Maybe he was tired, or discouraged, or maybe he believed, as she did, that they were rescuing injured people and giving them false hope.

"Make them bring help," he said. "No matter what Emperor Aetayn orders. Get someone to come in here and help us."

"I will," she said. "I promise."

17 hours, 32 minutes

Tuvok had left the bridge to investigate the shuttlebay personally. Chakotay was examining Starfleet protocol on dealings with prewarp cultures.

Janeway was studying the suns, watching the flares ripple off them like her own private fireworks show. So much beauty and so much destruction. It always amazed her that such things usually went hand in hand.

Her own console had the schematics for the alien vessel. It's name was *Traveler* and it was even more amazing than she had thought. Tom Paris's spit and glue analogy seemed even more apt when she saw what the aliens—who called themselves Rhawns—had dealt with.

The exchange of information had come with that price question again. She was getting a sense that Rhawn culture had a rather primitive economic base. She would wager that it was, or had been, a capitalistic society. When she had a chance, she would study that. It would make a difference in the ways she approached their emperor, Aetayn.

Aetayn had surprised her. He had curly purplish hair, which his skin tone and eye color matched. His face held a great intelligence, but it was tempered by youth. If he had been human, she would have thought him maybe twenty years old. She had no idea how to judge Rhawnian age, but his manner made him seem very young. And he wasn't as certain of himself as a world leader should be.

Or at least, her preconceived notion of what a world leader should be. And perhaps his lack of certainty was caused by the fact he was dealing with a situation completely outside his range of experience, perhaps even outside the realm of his imagination.

She knew better than to make that judgment.

The turbolift doors swished open behind her. Janeway turned slightly. Seven and Torres entered. Their heads were together and they were talking softly but with animation. Janeway was relieved to see that they weren't arguing.

She had thought they might, since she had assigned them to find a way to make B'Elanna's plan work.

"I trust you have something to report," Chakotay said, raising his head from his own work. He had commented quickly, probably to prevent conflict.

Janeway suppressed a smile. Chakotay was good at deflecting conflict. It was one of the many things she valued about him.

"We have found a solution," Seven said.

Some of the other members of the bridge crew

looked at her in confusion. Leave it to Seven to believe that whatever she was working on at the moment was the most important thing.

"You'll be able to push that ship without tearing it apart?" Paris asked.

"We found a way to make it work," Torres said as she approached him. She sounded surprised, although Janeway didn't know if she was surprised that the plan had worked, or that she and Seven had found a way to work together so quickly.

They had worked well together on other projects in the past, but they always sniped at each other. Perhaps this project had been done with a minimum of fuss.

"We *trust* it will work," Seven said, correcting her.

Maybe the fuss hadn't been at such a minimum after all.

"What have you come up with?" Chakotay asked. Janeway was content to let him take the point on this. She wanted to listen and evaluate anyway.

Torres and Seven looked at each other. Then spoke in unison.

"There is . . ."

"We have . . ."

They both stopped.

"One at a time would be simpler," Chakotay said. Janeway heard the undercurrent of amusement in his voice.

"Harry, can you give us a visual?" Torres asked Kim.

He replaced the image of the suns with that of the massive alien ship.

B'Elanna walked toward the screen and pointed to

a structure on the sunward end of the long ship. "This area holds the engines."

"Nuclear fission engines," Seven said. "Primitive and dangerous."

Very dangerous, Janeway thought. And much more unstable than she liked.

"If we install 'push points' on the sunward end of the ship, around this engine structure, we have a chance of moving the ship forward with minimal damage."

"Minimal damage?" Paris asked.

Janeway caught that phrase too, but decided not to follow that angle at the moment. "Explain the push points to me."

"We'll reinforce places on the ship's superstructure," B'Elanna said.

"Right now," Seven said, "the ship does not have the capacity to withstand the force of our tractor beam on any given point. If we install reinforced areas we are calling push points, using smaller tractor beams to tie parts of their structure more firmly together, the ship should be able to handle the stress of the increased pressure as we push it to increase its speed."

The plan seemed both sound and logical. And risky. But Janeway had known that any solution they came up with would have a level of risk.

"The problem is that they'll have to shut down their engines to let us install the push points." B'Elanna looked at Janeway as she said this, and Janeway immediately understood.

The Rhawns had no real reason to trust them yet. Janeway doubted the engines had been shut off since the journey began. Maybe one or two had been shut down at various times for repairs, but not all of them.

Getting permission from the Rhawns to do this would take diplomacy.

"How long will it take you to install these push points?"

"Four hours," Seven said.

"If nothing goes wrong," B'Elanna said.

Janeway nodded. "Then you had best get right on it."

"Seven and I will need some assistance on this," B'Elanna said. "I was hoping we could have Harry on our team as well as Ensign Vorik from engineering."

"Fine," Janeway said. "Give me some time to prepare the Rhawns. My best chance will be to do that in person."

"You aren't going alone, are you?" Chakotay asked so quietly that only Janeway could hear.

"Why?" she asked. "Does something about the Rhawns concern you?"

"Only the fact that we know so little about them," Chakotay said.

Janeway nodded. "I'll be bringing two security guards and Mr. Neelix."

"Guards?" Chakotay asked. "Does something about the Rhawns concern *you?*"

She shook her head. "But their leader calls himself an emperor. It suggests a hierarchy. If I go without the proper contingent, I might not get the respect I need. If I don't need the contingent, I'll be fine, but it's better to be prepared than not."

Chakotay nodded. "Do you think they'll go for this?"

"If they want to survive," Janeway said, "they have no other choice."

17 hours, 25 minutes

Thousands dead. Tens of thousands injured or homeless or both. The disaster on Unit 3 was catastrophic, and the figures were just now beginning to pour in.

Emperor Aetayn sat in his throne, thinking about the resources. They had found a way to close those holes quickly, and his engineers were taking care of the cracks in the hull. But he had assumed that Unit 3 would be able to handle its own wounded, just as the sections were supposed to do in each charter.

It had become clear that they couldn't.

He was silently berating himself. He should have seen it, just from the images he'd seen on the viewscreen. Parts of Unit 3 had been flattened. The hospitals near the site of the incident had been destroyed, and the medical personnel were probably dead.

How could he have thought the section had the resources to cope with the problems it faced? His slow actions might have cost hundreds more lives.

He winced. There should have been some sort of training manual for this job, steps that an emperor went through in each emergency situation. He wondered how many others he had missed in this instance.

He wondered how many his father would have missed. After all, no one in the history of his people had ever dealt with this kind of disaster.

Aetayn gestured toward Gelet. His assistant came toward him. "I am issuing Imperial Order Number 12546—we are on 546, aren't we?"

"Yes, Excellency."

"Then that's the order I'm issuing, declaring that the juncture points with Unit 3 are open for the duration of this emergency. Emergency personnel from all units connecting to Unit 3 may have unrestricted travel, so long as their papers are in order. By emergency personnel, I mean people with medical training, engineers, and all other jobs that pertain to the crisis."

"What about reverse flow?" Gelet asked.

Aetayn frowned. "Reverse flow?"

"Of the injured out of Unit 3. I doubt the hospitals in that section can handle them now. There will be a lot of movement between sections if you open this up."

But there would be more deaths if he didn't. He sighed. "I suppose it will work so long as everyone has their papers."

Gelet looked away. "Excellency, the citizens of Unit 3 have lost everything. I doubt most of them will have their papers."

It made for a logistical nightmare. Aetayn shuddered. In this case, he did know what his father would do. His father would have prevented the flow between sections, believing that the populations had to cope with their own problems in their own ways. The potential strain on the resources of the adjacent units might jeopardize more lives.

Aetayn was not his father.

"Tell all residents of the other units in that section to

carry their papers at all times. Then we will automatically know that those without papers are from Unit 3."

"Very well," Gelet said. "I will give the order immediately."

Aetayn did not respond. Instead, he leaned back in his throne. Perhaps he had not given the order before because before he had felt that his people might not survive the explosion of the suns.

The arrival of the aliens had changed that.

He still felt numb, as if his mind didn't quite work properly. Part of it was dealing with the fact that there were aliens—hundreds, maybe thousands, maybe millions of species of aliens—all over the universe. So many of them that they had divided space into quadrants and traveled through those quadrants the way his people used to travel over water.

The aliens were much more advanced than his people. He wasn't at all sure how to handle that. His rule was predicated on the idea that Rhawns were the supreme species, and his family the prime examples of it.

To have this basic tenant of Rhawnian philosophy upset would cause all sorts of disruptions in Rhawn society.

Everything was changing. There might be life after the explosion of the suns, but it would be a different kind of life, one he wasn't sure he was prepared for.

"Excellency?" Erese looked up from his console. "We are being hailed by the aliens. They seek permission to come aboard."

He went cold, then hot. Come aboard? How would they manage that?

"How many of them would like to join us?" he asked, keeping his voice calm.

"Only four."

Four held no threat that he could see. Even with superior weapons, they couldn't take over the ship. It was too large.

He was amazed his thoughts had turned in that direction, but they had. He knew so little about the aliens that he was afraid their generous offer was merely a ruse to get all the valuable resources off *Traveler.*

Or make a bid for *Traveler* herself.

"Tell them that I would be happy to meet with them," he said.

Erese nodded and moved his fingers along his console.

"Ask them how they plan to dock with *Traveler.* I'm not certain we can open our hatches. It's been—"

The air before him shimmered. He stopped talking, feeling slightly light-headed. He had stopped breathing as well. He raised his fingers to the bridge of his nose and rubbed the relaxation point. The movement helped him breathe, but it didn't stop the shimmer.

The shimmer grew brighter and brighter, then solidified into four beings, who stood before him.

The woman he had been dealing with—Janeway— stood directly in front of him. She was smaller than he had anticipated. If he stood, she would barely come up to his shoulder. The two creatures in the back were taller and looked stronger to Aetayn's inexperienced eye. The fourth being, a small male with mottled skin and wispy, hair stood at Janeway's side, wearing clothes far more lavish than the others'.

Janeway inclined her head, apparently in greeting. "Emperor Aetayn."

"Captain." He couldn't keep the surprise out of his voice.

"I don't know your greeting customs," she said. "Forgive me for not following your standard protocol."

She had materialized out of thin air and she was worried that she hadn't knelt before him? What kind of creatures were these?

"How—how did you get here?" For once his voice failed him. His entire staff was watching, and so were the rest of the command center personnel, although most of them pretended to be busy.

"We have matter-transmission technology. It allows us to beam from one place to another without using ships. Any other explanation would be too complex and time-consuming. Perhaps after we settle this crisis, we can show you how it works."

He nodded, not certain he wanted to know.

"Let me introduce my companions." She turned. "Beside me is our hospitality officer, Neelix. And two members of our security team, Ensign Lithadolous and Ensign Aris."

He focused on them. Ensign Aris's skin was blue—a bright blue.

"You are all of the same species?" he asked, knowing the question was rude, but unable to keep it in.

Janeway smiled. "No. We have representatives of many worlds aboard *Voyager*."

Many worlds. He was beginning to get a clearer picture of the universe.

"I would like to discuss our plans with you," she

was saying. "Would you like to do it here, or somewhere more private?"

"This is our command center," Aetayn said. "Nothing leaves this room without my permission. We will be able to have our discussion here."

Normally, in a diplomatic situation, he would have found a private room, had assistants with him and guards at the door. But this was not a normal situation, and he wasn't certain he wanted to be alone with these creatures. Not yet.

Janeway nodded, then looked about as if she were uncomfortable. Perhaps she was unused to looking up as she spoke. Aetayn was still in his throne, quite a bit higher than she was.

It was a small advantage, but he took it. He felt that he needed it more than he cared to admit to himself.

"We have checked and cross-checked our information," she said. "The suns will collide in less than twenty hours as you measure time."

"In other words," he said, "the explosion will happen soon."

"Very soon," she said. "If we leave you on your own, your ship will be vaporized. There will be nothing left."

All around him, he heard an outrushing of breath. He hadn't shared that information with much of his command crew. They had known the explosion would hit the ship, but not the final result. He had wanted to keep up the hope and drive in the command center. That, now, was gone.

Or maybe not. Maybe the aliens would provide it simply from their presence.

"Have you found a way to help us?" He sounded

desperate and he no longer cared. He *was* desperate.

"We think so," Janeway said. "We will use a tractor beam to push your ship forward, to give it enough speed to get it away from the explosion."

"I don't know what a tractor beam is," Aetayn said.

"It's one of *Voyager*'s many marvelous technologies," the little man—Neelix—said. He seemed inappropriately jovial. "I have gotten to experience many of those technologies over the years, and some of them still astound me."

Aetayn stared at him, not quite sure what the man's point was.

"Captain Janeway brought me along as a resident of this quadrant. I'm Talaxian. The captain found me years ago, and brought me on board as a kind of guide through my own region of space. So all of *Voyager*'s technologies were new to me once, rather like they're new to you."

He was a servant? Aetayn didn't understand why Janeway had brought a servant with her and then had let him speak.

"Mr. Neelix is one of our most valued crew members," Janeway said, obviously sensing Aetayn's discomfort. "He has quite an understanding of other cultures."

So he wasn't exactly a servant. Aetayn felt his shoulders relax. She hadn't affronted him after all.

"I was going to tell you about the tractor beam," Neelix said with that strange joviality. "It's a force beam that moves things across small distances in space. Kind of like a magnet works against metal. If you put out a pin and then use a magnet, the pin comes toward it. Only the tractor beam is much more sophisticated and versatile. It can—"

"That's enough, Mr. Neelix. I suspect you've given the emperor more information than he needs."

Aetayn was trying to imagine how such a beam worked. How such a beam could have been developed, and why such a beam would be necessary. But he was having trouble with it, just as he had trouble with many of the other concepts the aliens had introduced him to.

"You will focus this beam on us?" he asked. "And it will move us out of harm's way?"

"In a nutshell, yes," Janeway said.

He didn't ask what a nutshell was. He had a hunch he didn't want to know. "Are you asking my permission to turn this beam on us and push us out of the way?"

"If only it were that simple," Janeway said. "You see, your ship is much more fragile than the ships we're used to working with."

He thought of that sleek ship that he'd seen on his viewscreen. If all of their ships were like that, he understood what she meant.

"We're afraid, if we do this incorrectly, that your ship will come apart."

The tension returned. He let out a small *oof* of air through all of his airholes. The ones on his collarbone whistled slightly. Neelix jumped and looked at him as if he hadn't seen anything like it before.

"So," Aetayn said, "we either get vaporized or we run the risk of getting shaken into pieces that cannot survive on their own."

"Or," Janeway said, "you'll allow us to strengthen your ship."

He frowned at her.

"If my crew installs push points for the tractor beams, then your ship will be able to withstand the extra stress."

"What are push points?" he asked.

Janeway launched into a detailed description. He understood only every fifth word. Gelet seemed to understand more, because he nodded a lot from his position near Aetayn. Iquagt crossed his arms and frowned.

"Forgive me, Excellency," he said. "But I do not believe such things will make a difference. Our engines will continue to fire, our ship will continue to move. As they push, we will come apart."

Janeway looked at Iquagt with interest.

"Iquagt is my 'captain,'" Aetayn said. After the sentence came out of his mouth, he realized it was an acknowledgment of their different rank. Yet Janeway didn't seem to notice or care. "He knows *Traveler* better than he knows himself."

"He's right," Janeway said. "In order for this to work, you will have to shut down your engines."

"That's not possible," Aetayn said. "Those engines must remain on."

"Can't you start them again?" Neelix asked.

"Of course we can." Aetayn knew this because the engines had been stopped individually throughout the long journey. But while one engine was off, the others took its place. The engines were the most essential part of *Traveler*.

"Then I don't see what the problem is," Neelix

said. "Shut off the engines, let our people work on your hull, and then we'll push you to safety."

This was the moment Aetayn feared was going to come, the moment in which he would have to choose between what he knew and what he desired. He knew, from the nature of his own people, that beings encountering a lot of wealth—and *Traveler* had all of Rhawn's remaining wealth and resources— would perpetuate elaborate cons to gain that wealth.

If he shut off the engines, *Traveler* would be vulnerable. He would also lose any hope at all of getting away on his own. But if he did not, he might lose his people's only chance at survival.

Silently he cursed his father for leaving him alone to make this decision.

Janeway was watching Aetayn. Her face was filled with compassion—if he could read those unusually smooth features correctly—but she did not say anything. She was letting him make this choice on his own.

"If we allow you to do that," Aetayn said, "will we get away from that explosion?"

She nodded.

Then he had no choice, really. If he shut off the engines, and this alien crew raided *Traveler* for its resources, then his people would die. They would no longer need those resources. If he shut off the engines, and this alien crew got *Traveler* far enough away from the explosion, then his people would live.

It was that simple.

He turned to Iquagt. "Shut off the engines."

Iquagt stared at him for a long moment. Aetayn stared back. If Iquagt disobeyed him, Aetayn would have to have him arrested. Then he would need someone else to fly the ship, and there was no one else as qualified.

Everyone in the command center was staring at Iquagt. Aetayn could see the hesitation on all of their faces. He sensed that they wanted Iquagt to disobey him. They did not want to trust these aliens.

Then again, most of the command crew had not been living with the threat of total extinction for as long as Aetayn had.

Iquagt took a deep breath. Aetayn braced himself.

"Begin complete engine shutdown sequence," Iquagt said to his crew.

Murmurs of surprise rippled through the command center, but the staff complied.

The low background rumbling, the faint vibration in the floor and under his throne, that had been a part of his life for the past ten years suddenly faded and stopped.

For the first time in ten years, he remembered the sound of silence—and he realized he couldn't stand it.

17 hours, 20 minutes

Torres knelt in the engineering section of *Voyager,* checking her equipment for the last time. Each moment was precious. The quicker her team finished the work, the sooner they could try to get that alien ship out of the way of the explosion. And Torres had a hunch they would need all the extra time they could get.

Seven stood beside her, adjusting the front part of her environmental suit. She hadn't put on her helmet yet, and so she looked like she had gained an extra hundred pounds which showed everywhere except her face. And her hands, which weren't covered yet either.

Harry Kim was sitting on a chair near the rest of the suits. He was struggling to get his gravity boots on. He did this every time, and Torres found it annoying. She had a hunch he always took the boot one size too small, then couldn't get comfortable in them, and had to take out another pair. She didn't know if he did this because he couldn't remember his shoe size or if he simply believed he had smaller feet than he actually did.

Ensign Vorik was suited up and ready to go. His face was distorted inside the helmet, his features slightly extended. He swayed from foot to foot as if he couldn't believe that the rest of the team wasn't ready.

Torres wasn't ready at all. She hadn't even tried to put on her suit yet. She had a few other things to finish first.

"Seven," she said. "Get the coordinates for our position on that ship's hull, just in case."

"Just in case?" Harry said. "Just in case what?"

"You can never be too cautious," Torres said.

Seven went to the computer panel on the wall, and as she tapped it, the interface exploded, sending her flying backward. She slammed into the wall so hard that the back of her environmental suit made a loud, explosive crack.

Torres crouched. Harry hadn't moved, his boot still in his hand. Ensign Vorik had gone completely flat against the floor, as if he had been hit too.

But Seven had clearly taken the full force of the

explosion. The upper portion of her suit was blackened, the faceplate shattered.

The exploded panel exposed sparking and sputtering circuitry in the wall. "Computer," Torres snapped. "Cut power to the wall interface in this room."

With a tone of acknowledgment, the sparks died.

"Harry, see if you can figure out what happened to cause that panel to blow like that," Torres said as she hurried toward Seven. "Vorik, give him a hand."

Harry nodded to her, dropped his boot, and approached the panel as if it were a member of Species 8472. Vorik returned to his feet and joined him.

Seven's wasn't moving. Her fractured faceplate made it impossible to get a good look at her face, but Torres could see streaks of bright red clearly through it. She was afraid to risk removing the helmet.

Torres tapped her combadge. "Torres to bridge," she said, "medical emergency. Two to beam directly to sickbay on this signal."

Then she put her hand on Seven's shoulder. "You sure as hell better not die on me," Torres muttered to as the beam of light caught them.

Chapter Five

Lyspa set Andra down. Her daughter was heavy. She had become a deadweight halfway across the view-park, when the pain had made her pass out.

Lyspa had moved as fast as she could, stepping over downed trees, damaged furniture, and too many bodies. She hadn't realized how deadly much of the stuff in the park had been. Branches had impaled people, and the heavier items had simply crushed them. If she survived this, she knew what would be in her nightmares for the rest of her life.

But she had finally reached the door. The juncture door, so forbidden to enter without papers, had remained closed for the last seven hours, despite the nature of the emergency.

She had no idea how to open it. There didn't seem to be a visible knob from this side. Only a computer panel, and the panel meant there would be a code, a code she didn't have.

The last of the hope she was feeling faded. Amazing that it could be defeated by simple pale pink keys. There had to be another way in, otherwise there wouldn't be the strictures against crossing. She just didn't know what it was.

Then she felt something odd. For a moment, she didn't know what it was, but fear spiked through her body, making her very tense. Something had changed. Something important.

Everyone else in the park, everyone who was up and functioning and working, froze too. She wished Cyot were near her so that she could talk to him, but he was so far away she couldn't see him.

She couldn't see anyone she knew except Andra, whose precious face had turned a waxy lavender. Her daughter was going to die if she didn't get her out of here.

Lyspa stepped toward the door, and in that instant, she knew what was different.

The engines had stopped. The engines, which had sent them away from Rhawn, the engines which had saved their lives, and given them the opportunity to avoid catastrophe, had finally given up.

All of them. At once.

A shiver ran through her. That wasn't possible. There were redundancies upon redundancies upon redundancies.

Someone had shut off the engines. Emperor Aetayn, if he was still alive, had ordered them off.

Perhaps the disaster was wider spread than she had though. Maybe the end of her small corner of

Traveler had been the end of her people's escape to freedom.

Maybe.

The thought paralyzed her for an instant, and then she shook it away. She couldn't let herself think like that. She couldn't. Because if she did, she might let Andra die.

And Andra's death was impossible for her to face.

Lyspa touched the pink keys on the door. Maybe, without the engines, the juncture doors ceased functioning. Or maybe in this grave emergency, no one was monitoring them.

This might be her only chance.

She had to take it.

17 hours, 5 minutes

Seven of Nine's forehead was sore. It felt like she had been slashed with a knife. But she was careful not to wince as she sat up on the biobed.

"I have not given you leave to move," the Doctor said.

"Lieutenant Torres needs my assistance."

"I don't care if the creator of the universe needs your assistance," said the Doctor. "You don't move until I tell you to."

"I'm fine," Seven said.

"You're stubborn," the Doctor said. "That does not make you fine."

She glared at him.

"You nearly died from a concussion and a severe facial laceration. Fortunately for you, I've repaired both."

"Then I will no longer take up your time," Seven said. "My assistance is required on the mission."

She stood.

"Seven!" the Doctor said. "I was monitoring your blood pressure and heart rate. Sit back down so that I can finish."

"I will return when the away mission is over," Seven said as she headed toward the door.

"Take one more step and I will get Captain Janeway to take you off that mission," the Doctor said.

Seven continued forward. The captain needed her. Seven and B'Elanna Torres were the ones who knew how to put those push points onto the alien ship.

"Seven! I mean it!"

At that moment, the door to sickbay opened. Tuvok entered, completely blocking Seven from leaving. "Is there a problem?" he asked.

"Only that Seven of Nine is disobeying doctor's orders."

"Is that true?" Tuvok asked.

Seven raised her chin slightly. "I am fine."

"That was not my question," Tuvok said. "I was inquiring as to whether or not you were disobeying the Doctor's orders."

"I am needed on the away mission."

"I am not certain that is wise," Tuvok said. "Your health aside, your very presence may put the away team in jeopardy."

Seven frowned. "I am quite an efficient member of the team."

"I was not questioning your abilities," Tuvok said. "But someone is trying to kill you. We may assume that that person will try again when you are most vulnerable. And anyone in an environmental suit is extremely vulnerable."

"If you're going to have a long discussion," the Doctor said, "make Seven sit on the biobed. I can continue my readings."

Seven didn't even look at him. "We will not be having a long discussion. I will check my environmental suit. I will be extremely cautious."

"I trust you were being cautious earlier," Tuvok said.

"I am always cautious."

"And yet you were still attacked. I submit that in this case, caution may not be enough."

"And neither are proclamations that you're fine." The Doctor grabbed Seven's arm and tugged her in the direction of the biobed. She allowed him to move her, since she would now finish this conversation. Tuvok had gotten her full attention.

"They can't do this without me," she said.

"I suspect they can," Tuvok said, "but I do know that the captain would prefer to have you on the team."

Seven nodded. Then the back of her legs hit the biobed and she sat on it abruptly.

"If you cooperate with my investigation, then I will convince the Doctor to release you from sickbay so that you may go on the away mission."

"You do not have to convince the Doctor," Seven said. "I will leave whether he wants me to or not."

"You forget," the Doctor said, "I have the power to keep the captain here against her will. If I can do that to her, I can certainly do it to you."

"I am fine," Seven snapped.

"You're still bruised and your blood pressure is

slightly elevated. The readings suggest that you're in pain. Is that true?"

"No," Seven said.

"You're such a terrible liar, Seven," the Doctor said as he continued his examination of her.

"While he is doing that," Tuvok said, "I would like you to listen to the voices of the female crew members, filtered through the communications system. I believe, in this way, we shall be able to find your attacker."

The Doctor held the tricorder near her face. Seven pushed his hand away. "That will take too long."

"It will take less time than this argument has," Tuvok said. "I have isolated the crew members who were alone just before the attack in the shuttlebay. There are not that many of them."

Seven sighed. "Voices can be purposefully distorted."

"Yes, they can," Tuvok said. "However, doing this will eliminate the obvious, which is always the first step in an investigation."

"It'll also keep you here until I'm satisfied that you're healthy enough to go on that away mission," the Doctor said.

Seven crossed her arms. "You planned this."

"I would like to say that I'm that devious," the Doctor said. "Unfortunately, I'm not. Or I should say, I'm not—yet."

"All right," Seven said to Tuvok. "What do I have to do?"

"Listen carefully," Tuvok said.

Seven lay back on the biobed and closed her eyes. "You may begin," she said.

16 hours, 1 minute

B'Elanna wiped her hands on her uniform. She was too hot. The engine room—if you wanted to call something that big a room—of the alien ship smelled of hot metal and ancient grease. The temperature inside the room was about five degrees below unbearable. These aliens, these Rhawns, seemed to like things hot.

They also appeared to be masters of make-do engineering. When a part broke down, they seemed to find a way to fashion something else that worked almost as well. They had planned to crank up their engines, to run them at a hundred percent capacity, and it was lucky they hadn't. Many of the makeshift parts would have buckled under the strain.

But the primitive engines, silent now, weren't her concern at the moment. Instead, she was focusing on the even more primitive computer system before her.

Five Rhawn engineers hovered over her. They were all taller than she was, and they were all whip-thin. Most of them had callused hands and scarred faces from the work they'd done. But what unnerved her most was the various shades of purple that composed their skin.

She found purple aliens difficult to take seriously. She supposed it would be even harder for her if they were pink.

And she wasn't usually the type who let appearances affect her. But in this case, she couldn't get past her own prejudices. The lavender that shaded the chief engineer's face was the very color that Naomi Wildman had chosen for the girlish bedroom in her latest holodeck program. When B'Elanna, who had been helping Naomi set up the program, asked her if she was sure of the color, Naomi had smiled.

"Lavender is prettier than pink, don't you think?" she'd asked in that soft, excited voice of hers. "It's frilly without the frills."

The strange thing was B'Elanna had known exactly what Naomi meant. And she couldn't get the little girl's words out of her head while she worked with these aliens. Even their teeth were purple.

Purple People Eaters, Tom had said after he had seen the Rhawn emperor on the viewscreen. The entire bridge crew had looked at him in shock, but he had shrugged in that attractive devil-may-care way of his.

It's an old song from the mid-twentieth century, he'd said. *I'll play it for you sometime.*

I am sure that will not be necessary, Tuvok had said in reply, and the entire crew had burst into laughter. Tuvok had seemed confused.

B'Elanna had been amused, but for a slightly different reason. Tom's knowledge of the trivia of his people—centuries-old material—always startled her, and made her feel a little inadequate. She knew about the major things that every Klingon should know from Sto-Vo-Kor to the entire (doubtlessly mythologized) life of Kahless. But she didn't know the details—the popular music of Kahless's day, for example—and if truth be told, she didn't really care to know. It seemed like a waste of brain space to her, however attractive she found it in Tom.

She kept her head down now as she worked. The thought of the song and its goofy refrain—Tom had been kind enough (or mean enough) to have the computer play it for her before she left—ran through her mind. It was everything she could do to keep her attention on the task before her.

And she needed her full concentration. She had to install a computer program that would run the alien ship's steering jets efficiently. The jets had to keep the ship balanced so that it wouldn't get torn apart.

The Rhawn computer system was ancient. She hadn't seen anything that required input with keys in anything but a museum. The keys were covered with unfamiliar symbols, so she often had to ask the Rhawn engineers to help her.

She also found it slightly offensive that the keys were pink.

Cultural differences often bothered her, but never before had color been one of them. She wondered why she found colors in this spectrum so offensive.

The Rhawn engineers oohed and aahed every time she input more data. One of them exclaimed that he had never seen anyone work so quickly on a computer before. She had felt that she was going too slow.

Then she heard a faint hum and Seven materialized beside her. B'Elanna took a step back in surprise.

"I thought you were incapacitated."

"Sorry to disappoint you," Seven said as she studied the computer keyboard. "Primitive. Does it work?"

The Rhawn engineers who hadn't seen B'Elanna beam in had been startled by Seven's sudden appearance. Then, when she insulted their equipment, they looked offended.

"Yes, it works," B'Elanna snapped. "But I'm afraid our program might be too sophisticated for it."

"Let me." Seven bent over the keyboard and began to type.

"You don't know what you're doing," B'Elanna said.

"Of course I do," Seven said. "The Rhawn are Species 3105. Their technology is primitive, but familiar."

"How is that possible?" B'Elanna asked.

Seven gave her a cool look. "You do not want me to answer that here."

"What?" one of the engineers asked. He looked confused. "What did you call us?"

"Irrelevant," Seven said as she continued to type on the machine. Then she extended her hand. "Give me the program."

B'Elanna handed her the tricorder.

Seven sighed. "You expect me to input that with this?"

"Do you have another suggestion?" B'Elanna snapped. She hated it when Seven came late to a project and believed she knew everything about it.

Seven stared at the computer, then at the tricorder, as if just by looking at them she could make the technologies compatible. "No," she said after a moment, "I do not."

"Then let me," B'Elanna said. "I've been working on this. I'll finish."

"And then what?" one of the engineers asked as Seven stepped aside.

"Everything should work together," B'Elanna said, "once the program transfer is complete."

"You will have to monitor the system for overloads," Seven said. "We will only have a chance to do this once."

The engineer looked both surprised and uncomfortable. B'Elanna saw no reason to make him any more comfortable.

"Come on, Seven," she said. "We have work to do back on *Voyager*."

"I do not think we should leave this alone," Seven said.

B'Elanna hated baby-sitting technology while it did simple tasks. "We won't be leaving it alone. They'll be watching it." She nodded toward the engineers. "You'll contact me at the first sign of trouble."

"Absolutely," one of the engineers said.

"Good," B'Elanna said. "This might just go better than we expected."

15 hours, 48 minutes

Emperor Aetayn watched the events in the engine room with a feeling of discomfort. One of the aliens had "beamed" into the room without his leave. The guards he had posted outside the doors had known nothing about it.

He leaned back in his throne. The command center was a hub of activity, probably to cover the fact that the silence made most of the crew very nervous. He didn't like the engines being shut off either. He could feel his body straining for a sound that had once been a part of it, a sound that no longer existed.

With luck, he would hear it again.

He wasn't sure the aliens were going to bring him

that luck. Their ability to pop into and out of his ship without attracting any attention from his guards upset him. The aliens could "beam"—how accurate that word was—anything off *Traveler* and it would take him a long time to discover it.

They could even beam him off and no one would know where he had gone or how to get him back.

He still felt he made the right decision to allow these aliens to help him. But he could not bring himself to trust them completely. He was afraid they might do something to *Traveler*, to him, or to his people that would harm them.

Just not as much as the suns would.

He pressed a button at the base of his viewscreen, changing the image before him. His people had finally been able to get a visual from the points of impact in Unit 3.

Never in his life had he seen such devastation. Everything at the blast point was gone, blown into space. The edges were raw and jagged, covered with the second-skin material that seemed flimsy to his cursory view. But it was the emptiness that tugged at him. He hadn't seen emptiness like that in *Traveler* since he was a boy, touring the ship as it was being built. Only that emptiness had a clean newness to it, a sense of possibility.

This spoke of the lives lost, the homes gone, a part of his world that had vanished forever.

The death toll was rising. The minister of Unit 3 claimed she would have accurate numbers shortly. She was holding up remarkably well, considering her mate had been in the area when the asteroid had hit. He was missing, and presumed dead, like so many others.

Aetayn knew he would have to tour the devastation in person soon. But he wanted to wait until the crisis with the suns was past before he did so. He wasn't sure he could adequately deal with both emergencies at the same time. He was like those doctors in Unit 3, deciding which patient needed his fullest attention immediately.

He had to save the ship first and worry about one of its units second. No matter how guilty that decision made him feel.

15 hours, 18 minutes

Janeway sat in her captain's chair on the bridge, studying the long alien ship on the viewscreen. On the very back of the ship where the engines were, four small figures worked. Janeway couldn't make out which of those white suits contained Seven, Torres, Kim, or Vorik. Sometimes she thought she could tell from a movement, a gesture. But the lack of gravity distorted those movements and a moment after she was certain she knew, the feeling changed and she thought she might have been wrong.

Chakotay was monitoring the computer linkups that B'Elanna had set up. She had installed a program into the alien computer that would run the Rhawn ship's stabilizing jets. One of the features of the program was that it could be initiated from *Voyager*. B'Elanna had wanted to do that in case she couldn't make her wishes understood to the Rhawn engineers.

It seemed strange not to have Harry in his usual spot. The ensign who had taken his place was competent, but Janeway relied on Harry a lot more than she cared to admit. He was a natural at his work, which was one of the reasons she had sent him to the alien ship. He was trustworthy.

She was beginning to believe others on the ship were not.

It troubled her that Tuvok had not yet found the person who was trying to kill Seven. Tuvok had been studying all aspects of the attacks and so far had found nothing linking the attacks to any one crew member.

Seven had been unable to identify the mysterious voice that had summoned her to the shuttlebay. Unfortunately, she didn't rule anyone out either. As she pointed out to Tuvok, voices could be manufactured or disguised through the comm system. Just because she didn't recognize one of those voices didn't mean that one of them hadn't contacted her.

Tuvok had reported that last with a small degree of frustration. He had promised Janeway a report shortly, although he didn't sound as if he had a lot of solid evidence yet. And she wasn't even going to ask him about his hunches. He would claim he didn't have hunches, only possible scenarios based on fact.

Tuvok was also not on the bridge. A different security officer stood behind Janeway. It felt symbolic to her, that part of her bridge crew was gone. Symbolic of the way she had started feeling about the entire ship. Things were still familiar, but not entirely. It was as if she could no longer rely on anything she had once trusted.

These attacks on Seven were disturbing Janeway

more than she wanted to admit. She didn't like the way it made her feel about her crew, the way it made her feel uncomfortable in her own ship. If Tuvok didn't find the culprit soon, Janeway would start looking on her own. There had to be an answer, and she would find it—alone if she had to.

Tom Paris was watching the figures on the screen a little too much. The relationship between Paris and Torres never really bothered Janeway—she felt it softened B'Elanna and made Tom more involved with the ship—but every once in a while their feelings for each other would supersede their work.

"Ensign Paris," Janeway said. "Have you checked our readings lately."

Tom jumped—the movement was slight, but she saw it. Then he looked down at his board. "We're fine, Captain."

"Good. I'd like to make sure we stay that way. B'Elanna is in charge of the mission. Everyone will be safe out there."

Tom looked at her over his shoulder. "I hope so, Captain. With all the things that have been going on around here, I'm a bit worried."

It felt like he hadn't finished the sentence. *I'm a bit worried every time B'Elanna is near Seven.*

Janeway frowned. It was interesting that the two of them were together for two out of the three attacks. Were the attacks just leveled at Seven or was B'Elanna a target too? That would be something else to mention to Tuvok.

"Everything will be fine, Tom," Chakotay said. "As long as we cover our bases here."

Tom's lips narrowed. He clearly heard the rebuke.

Janeway half expected a sarcastic *Aye, sir!* but Tom restrained himself.

Janeway turned her attention to her command console. She tapped it, running the final calculations again and again. She wanted to know precisely what would happen when those two stars collided, and she wasn't satisfied with the answers she was getting.

They would be pulled into each other in approximately fifteen hours. Provided the alien ship hit the maximum speed B'Elanna felt it was capable of withstanding, the force from the explosion would still be intense. There would be an impact on that ship, whether they liked it or not.

Janeway had hoped they could keep it from being vaporized. But the impact of the explosion would be severe. Janeway wasn't sure that the fragile ship, its pieces linked together like rings on a bracelet, would be able to stay intact.

There were eight hundred million people and at the moment she didn't like their chances one bit.

14 hours, 21 minutes

Tuvok sat in his quarters going over his notes. He had narrowed the field to three suspects, all of them former Maquis. Of the three, only one seemed the most likely suspect.

Ensign Alery Matein had been in trouble before. On fifteen separate occasions, security had either been called to her quarters or interviewed her about an incident aboard ship. If *Voyager* had been able to stop at a starbase for routine maintenance, Ensign

Alery would have been one of the few crew members who would have been dismissed.

But *Voyager* did not have the luxury of dismissing difficult crew members and replacing them with new crew members from a starbase. *Voyager* had to find a way to make those crew members fit in. If that was not possible, then they had to make certain that those crew members caused a minimal amount of disruption.

In the past five years, Ensign Alery had received forty-five visits from security personnel, many of them surreptitious. Her personal logs had been reviewed by everyone on the security staff, including Tuvok himself. She had gone to special socialization classes with the ship's counselor, who, unfortunately, was also the ship's doctor, and she had received more than two dozen official visits from Mr. Neelix in his capacity as morale officer.

Each of those visits had resulted in good behavior for a time. But, if *Voyager's* maiden run had gone normally instead of the way it had, the report Tuvok wrote on stardate 48325.2 would have been filed with Starfleet. In that report, Tuvok had stated that he did not believe that Ensign Alery was Starfleet material and that her commission should be terminated.

He had believed that, as time progressed, Ensign Alery would grow into her job, but she was proving stubbornly unable to fulfill even the simplest of duties. The ship's morale officer had ordered her out of his kitchen—permanently. She took her meals in her quarters on most days, although she was allowed into the mess hall when the members of senior staff were present.

Her favorite holodeck program was a long-running bar fight that she often ran with the safety protocols shut off. When she had broken her arm for the third time, the Doctor contacted the captain, who ordered the program deleted. Three months later, Tuvok discovered that Ensign Alery had re-created the program, stored it under a different name, and continued to run it on the holodeck. For that infraction, her holodeck privileges were denied for a full year.

Ensign Alery had plenty of reasons to hate her confinement on *Voyager,* but try as he might, Tuvok could find nothing in her actions, in the ship's logs, or in her personal history to explain why Ensign Alery would take that hatred out on Seven of Nine. In the few times they had been together, they had treated each other cordially. Ensign Alery's experience with the Borg was limited to guarding one of the least important cargo bays during *Voyager*'s encounters with the Borg.

Indeed, only two things incriminated Ensign Alery: her inability or unwillingness to explain where she was when the attacks on Seven were made, and the conflicting stories she told when Tuvok interviewed her.

He was reviewing her interview on the computer in his quarters. He often went to his quarters while he was working, because they were quiet and he could meditate in peace. The interview had been brief.

He had frozen her image on the computer screen, studying her. She was Bajoran—comparatively small, as so many Bajoran women were, but incredibly tough and strong. She wore her Bajoran earring, the symbol of her religious faith, whose traditions she observed despite *Voyager*'s distance from her homeland. In those things, she was quite reliable.

It was her temper and her unpredictability that made her an unreliable officer. That, and her deep anger. Unlike most of the former Maquis on *Voyager,* Ensign Alery had never completely adjusted to her role as a member of *Voyager*'s crew. She had once accused Chakotay of betraying his Maquis roots, and when Torres became head of engineering, Alery hadn't spoken to her for nearly a month.

Tuvok's eyes narrowed as he contemplated that. There wasn't friction between Alery and Seven, but there had been quite a bit between Alery and Torres. Perhaps the attacks had been aimed at Torres and gone awry.

He considered the idea, decided it was worth pursuing, and then activated the interview. He started it in the middle, where her story diverged from the records.

His own voice filled the room. "According to our records, you were alone in your quarters when the second accident occurred."

"No." Ensign Alery's voice rose in irritation. "I told you. I was in the holosuite with Ensign Davis. Just ask him. We were running a new game program."

"I shall interview Ensign Davis," Tuvok said. "But be forewarned that records do not lie."

He had been implying, of course, that she might. Alery had caught the implication. He could tell it now as he watched her eyes narrow. He had made her angry. Of course, he had been trying to. Her anger was always the best weapon against her.

"I'm telling you the truth," she said. "When the first accident occurred, I was in engineering, monitoring the warp core, just like Lieutenant Torres told me to. The second time I was in the holodeck, and this last time, I was in the mess hall, trying to eat that slop Neelix calls food."

Tuvok frowned. He had found her repeated denials curious then, and he found them just as curious now.

"Ensign," he heard himself say, "do you understand the concept of an alibi?"

"I'm not making this up," she snapped. "You know, for all your pretense at fairness, Vulcans are among the most blind people I've ever known. I have no reason to lie to you. I have no reason to attack Seven of Nine, and I don't want to hurt *Voyager*. I'm not happy here, but I know that this is the only way I have to return home."

He hadn't responded, figuring that her words would hang her. Instead she had stood, the anger radiating off her.

"Commander, do you understand the concept of scapegoat? Because you are making pretty good use of it."

He froze the image now. It was logical to assume that because she had lied in the past, she was lying now. But in the past, her anger had always brought truth. Perhaps that was what had intrigued him about the interview.

"Computer," he said, "tell me the whereabouts of Ensign Alery on these occasions." He listed the times again.

It took only a moment for the computer to respond. During all three attacks, Ensign Alery had been alone in her quarters. Perhaps she had not worn her combadge. That would be consistent with her constant rebellion against authority. It would also explain why she was in one place and the computer said she was in another.

"Computer," he said, "on each occasion, how long was Ensign Alery in her quarters?"

"32.3 minutes, 45.6 minutes, and 22.4 minutes."

If she had refused to wear her combadge out of protest, then logically, she would have kept it off all day. But he had known for a long time that Ensign Alery was not always logical.

And if she had refused to wear her combadge, wouldn't she have told Tuvok this?

Perhaps not. Perhaps she had wanted to show him how flawed his reasoning was.

Tuvok pressed his own combadge. "Ensign Alery," he said.

Her response was immediate and sounded impatient. "Aren't you done with me yet, Commander?"

No matter how this situation resolved itself, her lack of respect would have to be reported to the captain. Tuvok made a mental note of it, not allowing himself to get sidetracked further.

"Ensign, at any time within the last week, have you failed to follow Starfleet regulations concerning combadges?"

"You really are fishing, aren't you, Commander? Violations of such minor regulations don't bring a jail sentence."

Tuvok made a second mental note about disrespect. "Just answer the question, Ensign."

"Of course not, Commander. If I'm going to violate a regulation, I'm going to violate one I can flaunt, one that will get me a lot of attention."

"Such as attacking Seven of Nine?"

"Are you going to press charges against me, Commander, because if you are, you need to inform me of it so that I can talk to you with some kind of counsel present." He heard the impatience in her voice.

"You have answered all of my questions for now," he said, and signed off.

Then he leaned back in his chair, templing his fingers, and contemplating what he had learned. He needed to look for common threads. One thread he had not completely explored was B'Elanna Torres. She had been present at two of the three attacks. Perhaps she was involved in some manner. Or perhaps she was supposed to be in the shuttlebay when Seven arrived.

The attacks might have been aimed at both of them.

"Computer," he said, "show me B'Elanna Torres's work assignments for the past week."

The work assignments would show what she was scheduled to do and what she actually accomplished. As the list scrolled before him, he saw nothing out of the ordinary. B'Elanna followed her assignments with precision.

She was also not scheduled to be in the shuttlebay at the time Seven was summoned there.

So much for that theory.

Tuvok leaned back, templing his hands again. So Lieutenant Torres was not a common factor. Seven of Nine was. There was also no record of any malfunction in the regeneration alcove or in the computer interface that had exploded. There was also no evidence of tampering with the computer system in the shuttlebay.

There should have been some evidence somewhere. Tuvok's frown deepened. Unless someone had tampered with it. He had kept the issue of tampering in mind while examining the crew. He had chosen only those crew members who understood the computer well enough to change its programming.

But he couldn't even find any record of them working on the computer system. No one had touched the computer system since Torres had replaced a gel pack on—

He whirled in his seat and examined the work log he had called up. Torres had replaced one of the computer's bioneural gel packs twelve hours before the first attack.

What if there had been no living agent at all? What if all of this had been caused by the computer itself? That would explain the lack of records, and the fact that no one had been seen in any of the attack areas in the hours before the attacks. It would also explain the discrepancies between Ensign Alery's story and the computer record of her whereabouts—although that seemed to be reaching.

Would a computer set up attacks and then frame crew members? Or were there other errors in all the files now as well, errors that would seem harmless unless held up to the cold light of an attempted murder investigation?

Perhaps the computer malfunction was causing it to see Seven's remaining Borg technology as some sort of threat. No one had started up her new alcove yet. The only functioning Borg technology on the ship, apart from her regeneration alcoves, was implanted in Seven herself.

And there had been no incidents in the last few hours, not since Seven had left the ship to work on the alien vessel.

Tuvok stood. The computer link in his quarters wasn't adequate for this investigation. He would need to go to the source.

Voyager's main computer core spanned three decks of the *Intrepid*-class starship. Virtually every system on board intersected within the massive artificial intelligence that kept the steady stream of automated functions and spontaneous human commands flowing to and from every part of the ship.

Autonomous self-maintenance meant it was only lightly staffed at any given time, barring a major malfunction or damage that required hands-on servicing by the crew. Tuvok passed only two crewmen as he entered the core and descended the gangway that led to the master records interface.

The computer had redundant records of its own operations, self-tracked by the nanosecond. Once he accessed those backups, he might gain more information, perhaps even detect a discrepancy that would explain what was really going on.

Tuvok stood in front of the interface console and realized his mistake half a second before it exploded. The blast lifted him up and away, throwing him across the room.

His last thought before blackness overtook him was that he should have first informed the captain of his suspicions.

Janeway stood, studying the viewscreen. The EVA team seemed small against the massive hull of the alien ship. They worked with almost Borg-like precision. Janeway smiled to herself. Seven's presence made itself known in very small, but very important ways.

Torres had just contacted *Voyager* to let it know that the push points were nearly installed. Within the next half hour, the EVA team would be back on board the ship.

Tom Paris had seemed relieved by the news, although he hadn't said as much.

"Captain," said Ensign Gilbert, who had taken Harry's position, "I'm registering an explosion in the computer core, at the master records interface."

Janeway turned toward her. "Another explosion? Is anyone hurt?"

"I don't know," Gilbert said. "My console isn't responding anymore."

Janeway returned to her chair. She tapped her own computer screen and got nothing. "I'm locked out."

"We all are," Paris said. "I can't get anything to respond."

"This doesn't make sense," Chakotay said. "The records interface isn't anywhere near the key control systems. Even if the whole room had been taken out, it wouldn't explain our consoles all crashing at the same time."

"Captain," Ensign Gilbert said, "our phasers are charging."

What the hell—? "Computer," Janeway said.

"This is Janeway Alpha Bravo One-Six-Eight-Five. Deactivate phasers. Repeat, deactivate phasers."

There was no response from the computer.

"Captain," Paris said, his hands flying over his console. "I think we've got trouble here."

Chakotay got out of his chair and hurried to Kim's station, pushing Ensign Gilbert aside. He worked furiously, but couldn't seem to do anything.

Janeway continued repeating her codes, but there was no response from the computer.

"Captain!" Paris pulled his hands off his console, holding them up like a little boy, to prove he had nothing to do with what was about to happen.

Phaser fire slashed across the viewscreen in front of her, smashing the alien ship right where the EVA team was.

"Chakotay," Janeway snapped. "Report."

But there was no report to be had. The computer had locked them all out. There was no way to get information. And from the image on the viewscreen, things looked bleak.

She could see damage on the hull, and no members of *Voyager*'s team.

She had no idea how they could have survived. She doubted they had.

"Captain," Tom Paris said, his voice shaking, "the weapons are powering again."

And there seemed to be nothing she could do about it.

Chapter Six

14 hours, 6 minutes

It had taken her much longer than she expected, but Lyspa finally got the juncture door open. She had managed to get through the computer security system (she had a hunch it had gone to default mode when the engines had shut off), and then she had to figure out how to open the door. It wasn't a simple twist-and-turn knob. Instead she'd had to find the latch, the handle, and the release. They all had to be worked at once before the door opened.

It had opened, revealing another door behind it. She wondered how many other doors she would find. She didn't like the prospect.

Andra was breathing shallowly behind her, her skin a sickly rose. Her daughter had never been this ill.

Others nearby watched as Lyspa worked. They

wanted to be able to get away if something happened to her, but she had a hunch they would help if she got inside. When she got the first door open, they had breathed a collective sigh of relief.

No one had been able to get through the main doors on the opposite side yet. At least the pile of bodies had stopped building. But the injured were getting weaker by the moment.

Including Andra.

The new door was protected by the same sort of computer lock. There was also a pressure and air monitor inside, apparently to let anyone know whether the juncture tube was attached on both ends. The monitors were in the black zone—safe—rather than the blue zone, which would have marked the emergency.

She did have a few worries, though. She thought she heard clanking on the other side. She hoped that part of the sounds were voices, but she couldn't be certain. She couldn't be certain of anything.

Still, she was going to open that door. She hoped that this computer code was as easy to open as the last one had been.

She wasn't sure how much time she had. Or, more accurately, how much more time Andra had.

She touched the keyboard, and as she did, the ship rocked again, extreme shuddery movements that nearly knocked Lyspa off her feet. People screamed. Andra moaned in pain and her eyes opened.

"Mommy?" she asked.

Lyspa crouched beside her. "It's all right, baby," she lied.

The rocking continued, as if a wave were flowing through the ship. Lyspa glanced at the door. The monitors had turned blue.

Their only escape route had just been cut off.

14 hours, 5 minutes

"We have confirmed this, Excellency," Gelet said. "That is weapons fire."

The viewscreens had gone out again. Aetayn cursed them and their fragility. Whenever there was a crisis, he couldn't see what was happening.

"Where is it coming from?" he snapped, whirling in his throne, wishing he had control of his own information.

"The alien vessel."

"Voyager?"

"Yes, Excellency."

"But didn't it fire at the engines compartment?"

"Yes, Excellency."

"Where its own people are working?"

"Yes, Excellency."

How could Gelet sound so calm? Everything had just changed. Their last chance had probably been lost.

If only *Traveler* had a viable external weapons system. The weapons they had wouldn't even get to *Voyager,* let alone do any damage. Aetayn wanted to fire back at them, to show them how it felt to be betrayed.

But his father would have said that reaction was childish. Aetayn had to take the upper hand.

Somehow.

"Contact *Voyager*," he said.

"We have a visual," Iquagt said.

That was quick. At least the viewscreens were working some of the time.

The image he received was of Captain Janeway. She stood in the center of her bridge, concern on her face. The man just before her, with strange yellowish hair, almost looked frightened. Aetayn found that curious.

"What kind of deception is this?" Aetayn asked. "You promise us help and then fire on our ship?"

"I apologize, Emperor Aetayn," Janeway said. "We're having a malfunction."

"Your malfunction could destroy *Traveler*."

"We're doing all we can, Emperor."

"Well, do more." He made an impatient signal with his hand so that Iquagt would shut down the communications.

The screen went dark.

"Your Excellency," Erese said, "the vibrations are causing problems at the juncture points."

"They weren't properly stabilized after the last explosion."

As if there had been time.

"Fire thrusters," Aetayn said.

"We are," Erese said. "They're enough for the moment. But if *Voyager* continues firing on us, the jets won't be able to keep up."

Aetayn cursed again. Why had he thought things happened slowly in space? Everything had changed in a moment—and he was now convinced his people would die.

14 hours, 4 minutes

The phaser fire was blinding up close. Seven of Nine felt herself get tugged over the edge of the engine section of the alien ship's hull. For a moment, her boots rose above the metal surface and she ran the risk of floating off into space.

But a hand held her tightly, pulling her to safety. Or relative safety.

She thought she heard a scream echo in the comm unit of her suit, but she couldn't be certain. Everything happened much too fast.

Her boots caught the metal side behind a small chimney-like feature. She had no clue what the feature actually was, only that it momentarily protected her from the phaser fire.

Then she looked at the hand, following up the arm to the helmeted face of B'Elanna Torres.

"Saving your life is becoming a habit," Torres said.

"I will endeavor to be more appreciative," Seven said.

"And more careful."

Phaser fire hit the hull again, shaking them and leaving scorch marks. Soon it would go all the way through, and no matter what Seven and Torres did, it wouldn't matter. The phaser fire would hit those primitive atomic engines and the explosion would take out both ships.

"That's *Voyager* shooting at us!" Torres said.

"I suspect it's shooting at me," Seven said calmly.

"Who are you, now, Tuvok?"

Seven ignored the question. She couldn't see Kim

or Vorik. She remembered that faint scream and wondered what had happened.

Another shot shook them.

"They're not going to stop," Torres said. She hit her combadge. "Torres to *Voyager*, what is—"

Seven pulled her hand away, severing the link. "Don't do that. If they know where we are, they'll be able to lock—"

Too late. The next shot was very close. Seven looked around, trying to see any way to get out of phaser range. Then she saw a metal ring a few meters from her.

"Come with me," she said to Torres, tugging her arm.

Torres apparently saw the ring as well and knew it for what it was: an old-fashioned hatch. "What about Harry and Vorik?"

"I don't know," Seven said. "I haven't seen them."

And that concerned her. They should have been right nearby. They had been when the shooting started.

Another burst of phaser fire, this time farther away. Whatever was causing the shots—whoever was causing the shots—apparently didn't know where Seven was.

She crouched, careful to keep the sole of her boots on the metal surface, and tugged on the ring with both hands. Torres crouched beside her. There had to be some sort of latch, something that Seven had missed, because the ring wasn't moving.

They couldn't open it.

Another phaser blast rocked the hull. Seven glanced toward the spot the shot hit. At least the phaser fire wasn't focusing on one area. If it had, there would already be a hole in the engine room's hull.

Torres cursed and then pulled out her own phaser. "Stand back," she said.

"I think we should attempt to open this without firing," Seven said.

"I think we should too," Torres said, "but I don't think we have the time. Unless you plan on dying out here."

Seven didn't answer. Instead she took two steps backward.

Torres shot at the hatch, burning a hole through the metal. Seven frowned.

"What was your phaser set on?" she asked.

"High," Torres said, grabbing the ring and pulling. This time the hatch opened.

She slipped inside.

Seven followed. Torres pulled the hatch closed, but she knew it wouldn't stay.

"Now what?" she asked.

"Let's hope they have redundancies," Torres said, "because I can't shoot in here."

"Here" was a narrow access tunnel, not unlike a Jefferies tube. Seven was clinging to ladder rungs and so was Torres. Seven held the hatch, studied its interior side for a moment, then found what she was looking for. Something simple, something old-fashioned. Something perfect.

A bolt. It clearly hadn't been used in years.

"Hold this." Seven indicated the hatch's hand-hold. Torres reached up and grabbed it. Seven took the slider on the bolt and shoved it into place.

An old-fashioned bolt lock. Seven looked at Torres, who grinned back.

Then the entire tunnel shook as another shot hit outside.

Seven slipped down several rungs, saved from any serious damage by her suit. Torres followed her down.

The shaft was dark and musty. It clearly hadn't been used in years.

"Why did you want to know about my phaser?" Torres asked.

"Because," Seven said, "if you could cut through the metal on that hatch with your phaser on high, then why weren't the shots from *Voyager*'s phasers cutting through the hull too?"

"Good question." Torres was silent for a moment. The only sound Seven heard was their boots clanging on the rungs as they continued to climb inside the ship. "I suppose you have a guess."

"I think it more than a guess," Seven said.

"Well, are you going to share it or do I have to pry the information out of you?"

Seven had reached the bottom of the shaft. It was blocked by what seemed to be a manually operated airlock. A wheel to one side allowed them to slide open the airtight outer door with little trouble. Once inside, they were able to close the hatch by way of a matching wheel on the other side. Torres found and activated a pressurization system, filling the airlock with atmosphere. Now, at least, they wouldn't have to worry about venting the ship's atmosphere through the preposterous access tunnel.

The inner door was in the floor of the airlock, narrow, and was obviously more sophisticated than the outer one, computer-locked and operable only from the other side. Torres found an access panel, exposed some wiring, and went to work.

"I don't believe *Voyager* is deliberately targeting the alien vessel," Seven said.

"You said that already. You think this is aimed at you."

"Yes."

"What does that have to do with the strength of the phaser fire?"

"Like all the other attacks," she said as she traced the thin wires, "this seems well thought out."

"How does it seem well thought out?" Torres asked.

"Why damage the alien vessel when I am outside of it? Why not hit me with phaser fire strong enough to knock me off my feet and away from the vessel, maybe even strong enough to kill me? You won't be able to reach me in time and neither will anyone from *Voyager*."

"Don't be ridiculous," Torres said as she worked. "If you were floating away in space, someone on *Voyager* would just beam you aboard."

"If they could," Seven said. "We don't know what circumstances precipitated this attack. The captain wouldn't allow the phasers to fire on us, if it were within her power to prevent it. Therefore something must be wrong on *Voyager*."

Torres stopped and studied Seven for a moment. "You really believe this, don't you?"

"Yes," Seven said. "Of course. It's the only reasonable explanation. Even if the Rhawns suddenly posed a threat, Captain Janeway would have beamed us back before commencing any attack."

"What if she couldn't wait?"

"She would have warned us, allowed us a chance to save ourselves. And she would have targeted the fire better."

Torres nodded, then returned to work. "All right. You've convinced me. So what next?"

She touched two of the wires together and a click echoed in the small space. The door slid partially open.

"You seem to have answered your own question." Seven pushed the hatch open and stepped through the rounded opening. There was a floor just a few meters below her feet. She jumped down and landed in front of six Rhawns.

They were not the ones she had seen in the engineering compartment earlier. In fact, they seemed quite young. All of them were male and all of them had a deep purple complexion and white hair.

They stared at her with their mouths open.

Then Torres landed beside her, and the boy closest to Seven screamed.

"Great." Torres pulled her helmet off and tucked it under her arm.

Three of the boys took a step backward. A man who also had deep purple skin, and who seemed to be wearing a uniform of some sort, hurried over.

Seven reached up and slammed the hatch door closed.

"Do you get the sense," Torres asked softly, "that they have no idea who we are?"

"Sometimes," Seven said dryly, "your logic is impeccable."

Torres held up her hands in a we-mean-no-harm gesture. "Hi," she said. "My name is B'Elanna Torres. I'm from *Voyager,* the ship that's been trying to help you."

The man stared at her. "What are you?"

"Take off your helmet," Torres whispered at Seven.

Seven did, just as the ship was rocked again. The boys tumbled in all directions, but the man managed to hold his ground. "My designation is Seven of Nine."

Torres sighed. "And lighten up a little. You're intimidating them."

"I believe *we* are intimidating them."

The rocking stopped and the boys stood.

"What's going on?" the man asked.

"It's too complicated to explain easily," Torres said. "Are you one of the engineers?"

"I'm the head of the engineering department on the campus at Section 6. I brought the boys here to study the silent engines."

"This is not an appropriate place for children," Seven said. What were these people thinking?

"We're not children," one of the boys said.

"You are certainly not an adult." Seven arched her eyebrow at the man. "Are there any engineers nearby? They will know what is going on."

The man studied her for too long a moment, then walked toward the wall. He pressed a button on it and static mixed with feedback echoed in the large space.

"I'm looking for Tatia," he said. "We need her in the computer room."

"The computer room?" Torres asked. "Where exactly is that?"

"Right here," one of the boys said.

Seven raised an amused eyebrow at Torres. She could already feel the beginnings of Torres's quick Klingon temper start to rise.

"No," Torres said. "Where is it in relation to the command center?"

"The command center?" The boys all looked at each other as if they had never heard of it.

Torres's eyes narrowed. Seven watched, her amusement growing. "You know," Torres said, "where the emperor is."

The boys made a strange gesture with their hands and then fell to their knees. They prostrated themselves.

The man frowned at her from the intercom. "You should not speak so casually of our leader."

"Well, he's not *my* leader—"

Seven elbowed Torres. "She meant no harm. We must visit the people who are running your ship. Time is of the essence."

A slight Rhawn whose lavender skin and dark magenta hair were in complete contrast to the men's skin and hair entered from a side door. She stopped, stared at Torres and Seven, and let out a whistle. "So you are the aliens I've heard so much about."

"Yes," Seven said. "We have an emergency. We would like to visit your command center."

The boys slowly rose to their knees and dusted themselves off, apparently realizing no more blasphemy was going to come out of the lips of these strange women.

"You're welcome to go," the engineer said, "but it is going to take you a while."

"How long?' Torres asked.

"If you hurry," the engineer said, "in two days."

"Wonderful," Torres said. "And we can't even ask *Voyager* to beam us over there."

"No, we cannot," Seven said. "It would seem that we are on our own. And whatever we do, it's going to have to be from here."

14 hours, 1 minute

Tuvok felt himself come to. It was a detached feeling, as if part of him had been conscious the entire time. He kept his eyes closed for a moment, just in case the computer had been monitoring him. He endeavored to keep his breathing the same and to make no outward sign of his growing wakefulness.

His body ached in various places—probably from the fall. The back of his head ached the worst; he had, apparently, hit it against the wall. His hands throbbed, a feeling he recognized. They were burned. How severely, he did not know.

He took the pain, made it into a separate entity, and forced it to one side of his brain. He would be able to function better without the pain influencing him.

Then he slowly opened his eyes.

The records interface was a blasted ruin.

Now what? Clearly this explosion had not been an accident. This incident and those that preceded it had been initiated by the ship's computer itself, although for what reason, Tuvok couldn't even speculate. He'd originally suspected that some glitch was causing it to seek out and destroy Seven's Borg technology, but the attack on him, at the precise location where he might obtain some answers, suggested there was something else going on.

He still believed that the problem could be traced back to Torres's routine swap-out of a bioneural gel pack, only twenty-two hours ago. If that was true, he might be able to isolate the cause of the problem . . . if he could get away with just one of the packs.

The question was, would he survive the attempt? Tuvok rose slowly off the floor, slipped out the room and up the rungs of the gangway without further incident. The two crewmen he'd passed earlier were nowhere in sight. Whether they were injured, dead, or simply elsewhere, Tuvok didn't know, and unfortunately he couldn't spare the time to find out. If what he suspected proved to be true, the entire crew was now in danger.

Lieutenant Torres would be better at this, of course. She knew more about the computer than Tuvok did. She would have been able to attack it with sureness and finesse. He, on the other hand, might have to resort to something he disliked—brute force.

Tuvok slowly entered the main bioneural circuitry bank, dozens of gel packs plugged into the complex system. Although the gel packs were distributed fairly evenly throughout *Voyager,* here at the core was the most dense concentration.

Apart from the usual blinking operation lights, everything was still. But that meant nothing. The records interface had looked similar before the explosion. On the other hand, the computer might not be willing to risk damaging components that were vital to its operation—such as the gel packs.

Tuvok calmly reached toward the nearest gel pack and tapped in the release command into the controls below it.

Nothing happened. He wasn't surprised.

He would only get one chance at what would come next, and the odds of his success were low. But he didn't hesitate. Tuvok drew his phaser, set it on high, and took precise aim at the locking mechanism holding the gel pack in place, tapping his combadge as he cut quickly through machinery.

"Tuvok to Captain Janeway."

"Go ahead." The captain's voice sounded distant. Tuvok hoped he had her and not some computer facsimile thereof. As far as he could tell, the computer had not reacted to his attack.

"Captain," Tuvok said, "our foe is no intruder. The computer is malfunctioning. It has just attacked me. I believe the problem is with the bioneural circuitry, and am attempting to retrieve one of the gel packs now."

"That explains why we've lost control of our weapons systems," Janeway said. "*Voyager* has opened fire on the Rhawn ship. We'll send someone to help you, Tuvok."

"Do not," Tuvok said. The phaser had finished its work. Tuvok reached out and ripped the gel pack free from its socket. "My task here is nearly done. I will be in touch shortly. Tuvok out."

Weapons. It went counter to Tuvok's instincts to leave *Voyager* defenseless, but the computer was giving him little choice. Without hesitating, Tuvok reset his phaser and fired again, this time burning through a bank that housed the specific ODN relays connecting the computer core to the ship's tactical systems. The damage wasn't irreparable, but it was disabling.

Tuvok ran toward the nearest Jefferies tube, still clutching the gel pack. He removed his combadge as he went and tossed it away so that the computer couldn't easily track him. But as he did, the wall next to him exploded.

13 hours, 59 minutes

Traveler continued to shake. Aetayn clung to his throne, feeling his anger grow. Janeway had promised him that this was a fluke, that it would ease, and it had not.

He was beginning to think that she lied.

"Your Excellency, the firing has ended." Iquagt delivered this news as if it were a death sentence instead of something to be pleased about.

Aetayn stood, a bit unsteady on his feet. The shaking was more of a vibration as the power of the shots made their way through the ship.

The command center crew watched him as if afraid of his reaction. He said, "How severe is the damage?"

"We do not yet know, Excellency," Iquagt said. "We can't send anyone to assess the damage."

"There are reports of aliens inside the ship," Gelet added. "They may be sabotaging the systems."

"May?"

"The report stated that they were tampering with computer technology when they were found."

Aetayn clenched his fist, resisting the urge to rub

the pressure points beside his nose. This time, he had to let the anger build. It was the only way to deal with Janeway.

What was her game?

"Find the aliens," he said. "Hold them until we know exactly what their captain is up to."

"Yes, Excellency." Erese was the one who responded. He bowed slightly. Aetayn sensed Erese's frustration matched his own.

Aetayn took the steps down from his throne and walked to the large viewscreen, staring at the image of *Voyager.* She was so much smaller than his ship— like an insect against a mountain—and yet she was so much more powerful.

Well, he hoped Janeway valued her crew members. Because Aetayn would take any advantage he could find. He might not have superior weaponry, but he had a superior mind.

It was time he used it.

13 hours, 57 minutes

For the twentieth time, Janeway tried her override commands. The computer was not responding.

But Tuvok had managed to do something. The phaser fire on the alien ship had stopped, leaving scorching damage on the Rhawn ship, and no sign of Kim, Vorik, Torres, or Seven.

It also seemed, although she couldn't be certain, that the team's work on the push points had been in vain. The computer had targeted those areas on the alien vessel, effectively ruining them.

Even if Janeway solved *Voyager*'s problem, she

had no idea how she was going to save the Rhawn vessel now.

Chakotay was at Tuvok's station, trying to find a back door into the computer. Paris was underneath flight control, attempting to disengage the computer from the conn.

Janeway didn't give those options much chance of working.

Finally, in exasperation, she put her hands on her hips.

"Computer," she said, "what the hell are you doing?"

The entire bridge crew stopped work and stared at her. She didn't usually swear on duty. She rarely swore at all. But her frustration was as plain as theirs.

"Please rephrase the question."

The computer's inflectionless female voice made Janeway start. She hadn't really expected an answer.

"Computer this is Captain Janeway. Explain your actions."

"*Voyager*'s computer is following its mission directive to safeguard Federation interests and eliminate threats to those interests."

Paris climbed out from underneath the navigational station. Chakotay whistled softly. But their surprise was nothing compared with Janeway's.

"Computer, explain. Identify the mission directive."

"Directive P1/OR-01047."

Janeway had never heard of it. "Computer, describe the nature of the threat."

"Seven of Nine."

Janeway swallowed. If she hadn't been living a nightmare these last few hours—and if there hadn't been so many attempts on Seven's life—she wouldn't have believed any of this.

Chakotay placed his hands flat on the console, clearly as stunned as Janeway.

Janeway considered her next question. She asked, "Who authorized this directive?"

"Ensign Roberta Luke."

It took Janeway a moment just to get past the word "Ensign." A simple ensign shouldn't have been able to override any of the computer codes, or the redundant systems in place to prevent such takeovers.

But once Janeway got past that word, she was even more stunned. Roberta Luke had been dead over eighteen months, ever since the encounter with the Srivani.

Janeway in her ready room, sleepless for days, her dopamine levels catapulted almost to insanity-producing levels by the Srivani's callous medical experiments on the ship's crew. Then the call from the bridge, Ensign Luke writhing in agony on the floor, dying of more physiological breakdowns than the Doctor could keep up with, Janeway's own attempts to resuscitate her in vain—

"Ensign Luke," Chakotay said softly, "specialized in the ship's bioneural circuitry."

Janeway looked at him and nodded. She had just remembered that. And she had remembered that at her funeral, almost everyone on the ship had described her as a loner.

But she's dead. Dead and gone for more than a year!

A dead loner who was trying to kill Seven and, unless Janeway regained control of *Voyager*'s computer, might kill the rest of the crew as well, along with eight hundred million other souls.

"Computer," Janeway said, "this is Captain Janeway. Abort Directive P1/OR-01047. I say again, abort Directive P1/OR-01047. Accept command override Janeway Theta One."

But the computer said nothing more.

Chapter Seven

13 hours, 47 minutes

Lyspa sat on the floor, staring at the juncture door monitor, her arms around her daughter. Andra was slipping in and out of consciousness, moaning with pain. Lyspa kept smoothing the hair off her daughter's forehead, thinking of all the sacrifices she and her husband, Onsflet, had made so that her daughter would grow up, live a full life, and have children of her own.

That dream was dying now with Andra, and so was the meaning of all the sacrifices—of Onsflet's sacrifice, staying on Rhawn because they couldn't afford passage for him, Lyspa, and their unborn child. Besides, his skills weren't considered necessary for Rhawn survival.

Hers were.

She thought that such an irony now.

The monitors were still blue and the ground continued to shake. The pounding behind the juncture door had grown even louder—it was almost a ringing sound now—and Lyspa wondered if that door would blow open soon, revealing a ruptured juncture that would suck them all into space.

There had been a huge cheer from the other end of the viewpark only a few moments ago. From what she could tell, someone had cleared a small path out of the viewpark and they were sending for help.

She had a hunch that help wouldn't be arriving any time soon. If the viewpark was the only place affected, maybe someone would come, but she knew that something worse had happened on the other side of the main doors. She had felt the change in pressure. She had seen the emergency repair vehicles.

Something awful had happened there, and most of the emergency personnel—if they survived—were probably already too busy to come to the viewpark.

The pounding grew even louder. Lyspa tightened her grip on Andra and watched the juncture door.

Suddenly, it sprang open, and a woman toppled out.

She was wearing the palest lavender-blue, a color reserved for emergency personnel only. Lyspa blinked, thinking this a vision. Another woman crawled out of the door, and then a third, followed by two men who were dragging some equipment.

"That was close," the first woman said as she got up. She saw Lyspa, noted Andra, and smiled. "Hi. We're the first, and probably only—at least for a while—emergency team from Unit 2. I thought we were going to be stuck in that juncture forever."

She crouched beside Andra, put a hand on her head, and then took a pulse.

"First critical," she said to the others. "We need some fluids and replacements immediately."

The other two women surrounded Andra, somehow easing her out of Lyspa's grasp. She watched with both fear and gratitude as they started tending her daughter.

After a moment, the first woman's words registered in Lyspa's brain. "What's wrong with the juncture?"

One of the men answered. "It's holding together all right, I think. But there's something huge happening out there, shaking the entire ship. When that happens the junctures seal off. I have no idea how we even got out. Your door should have been locked."

It had been, but she had unlocked it. She had brought them in here, maybe even saved their lives.

Maybe, they would save Andra's life in return.

But she wasn't going to confess to violating the law. "Maybe something knocked it loose," she said, but he was already moving away from her, off to save other lives.

13 hours, 47 minutes

Tuvok slipped out of the Jefferies tube into engineering. He avoided the worst of the blast in the computer core by diving into the tube, but the burns on his face were distracting. He accepted the pain, and put it aside. Fortunately he had kept the gel pack safe, hoping it would reveal something about how all this came about, and how it might be brought to an end.

Tuvok glanced around. The warp core continued its normal pulse, adding its distinct colors to the entire deck, but he was alone. There should have been a staff complement of at least ten engineers, but there were none. He scanned the floors to see if the staff was lying on them, unconscious, but they were not.

Engineering was empty.

That explained why no one had been working at defeating the computer from this end.

Except for the hum of the warp core, this room was extremely quiet.

Tuvok hurried to the main computer interface and began to work. From the information on the screen, he saw that the computer was still dealing with the problems he had caused in the core. So he had a little time.

He'd had a chance to go over his plan while he was in the Jefferies tube. He had devised a diversion, one that would only take a few moments to implement, and would keep the computer occupied even longer.

If it did not succeed he would then disable the computer's higher cognitive functions. The computer would still be able to continue running *Voyager* on a basic level, but would not be able to make its own decisions per se. The ship would be much harder to handle and maintain with its artificial intelligence effectively lobotomized, but the current danger would be eliminated.

Saving the Rhawn might be even harder, but still possible . . . *if* Tuvok could carry out his plan in time.

13 hours, 45 minutes

A two-day walk. Or run, depending on what that Tatia had meant. Either way, it was much too long.

Torres made her way through the twisting corri-

dors of the massive alien ship, wondering how anyone survived in this rabbit's warren. Seven followed
closely behind, along with the Rhawn engineer, the
teacher, and his students.

Torres felt like the Pied Piper, only she wasn't trying to lead. She wished the Rhawns would leave her
alone. But she and Seven were curiosities and, after
eight years in space, the Rhawns didn't have many
of those.

She had tried to contact Harry twice and Vorik
once, but she hadn't gotten any response. And that
worried her more than she wanted to admit.

The corridor ahead of her split in three different
directions. No one had had a map of the entire ship—
apparently no one in her little band ranked high
enough to be able to request one—so she had had to
rely on instinct. Only instinct wouldn't help her here.

"All right," she said, pulling up short. "Which way
out of this part of the ship?"

She had turned around as she asked the question
and she found herself staring at wide, shocked eyes.
She shook her head slightly—they had known why
she and Seven wanted the information. Were they all
dense?

"Come on," she snapped. "Tell me where we go."

"It would be in your best interest to cooperate,"
Seven said in her most menacing tone. Torres had to
admit that having Seven at her side in an emergency
was a Very Good Thing.

Tatia licked her lips. "We, um, don't leave this
part of the ship."

"Oh, you live in the atomic engines?"

Tatia flushed a deep maroon which clashed with

her hair. "No. We have living quarters. But they are in this section. You cannot go from unit to unit without express permission of the emperor's staff."

"Or papers," one of the boys said. "Some people have papers."

"Well," Torres said, "we're not part of the crew, so we don't need papers or permission. We're going. Just tell us which corridor to use."

The group behind them exchanged glances. She had a bad feeling about their response.

In unison the boys pointed at the left-hand corridor. The adults pointed to the center one.

"All right, Seven," Torres said. "Let's go."

She marched down the right-hand corridor. Seven caught up to her and whispered, "They did not indicate this direction."

"I know that," Torres said. "But they also told us it was illegal to leave this area of the ship. You think they're going to tell us how to break their laws?"

"I follow your reasoning. It is surprisingly logical."

Leave it to Seven to make a compliment sound like an insult. Torres marched on, wishing she had brought emergency rations, or at least a bottle of water. She had a hunch this was not a place where she could rely on the kindness of strangers.

She reached a large door. Behind her, she heard a collective gasp, which made her feel that she was on the right track. Seven wrapped her hand around the knob.

"Stop!" Tatia said. "It's a forbidden area."

Torres smiled at her. "Guess you're all just going to have to stay behind. Thanks for the escort."

Then Seven pushed the door open. She and Torres

entered. The boys, their teacher, and Tatia remained outside, looking very flustered.

Torres pulled the door closed, then turned around, nearly crashing into Seven. Seven held her back with one hand. In front of them were some Rhawns in matching black uniforms, holding knives on two people.

Two people wearing EVA suits.

Harry and Vorik.

13 hours, 45 minutes

It made no sense. Even if Ensign Roberta Luke was an engineering wizard, which she decidedly had not been, she could not have gained control of *Voyager* when she was alive, let alone after death.

The computer was going through a serious malfunction. Perhaps akin to having a human being go insane—bits and pieces of information were rising to the surface in orders that made no sense. At least, that was what Janeway believed. She honestly didn't know what else to think.

She'd tried to verbally engage the computer for ten minutes after the computer had mentioned Luke, but it remained unresponsive. Chakotay reported that several key command pathways had been compromised, and the computer was attempting to repair them.

For that, Janeway silently thanked Tuvok, and hoped he was safe. He wasn't answering his combadge.

"Captain," Chakotay said. "I'm getting a communication on a radio frequency."

"Radio?" She walked to Chakotay's station and looked down. Sure enough, information was coming across a broadband, the way it did four centuries ago. "Can we access it?"

"I think so," Chakotay said. "It seems to be in one of the very few systems the computer hasn't locked off."

He pressed the console and Tuvok's voice filled the bridge.

"Captain, I am contacting you because we must communicate and I do not believe we will get another chance."

"Can we answer him?" Janeway asked.

"I don't know," Chakotay said. "I have no idea how to communicate this way."

"I do." Paris slid out from underneath the flight control station. "Just give me a second, Captain."

He climbed into his chair, worked his fingers over the console, and then said, "Go."

"Tuvok, can you hear me?"

"Affirmative."

"Where are you?"

"Engineering," Tuvok said, and Janeway felt her shoulders relax slightly. "I am, however, quite alone. I do not know why."

Neither did she. "Are you able to isolate the problem?"

"I believe so, Captain. I am going slower than others would, as I am no expert in this matter, but I seem to be resolving some of the major issues. However, my task would go quicker if the Doctor could join me."

"The Doctor?" Janeway asked.

"Yes. I believe the cause of the computer's aberrant behavior is something that has been genetically encoded into the ship's bioneural circuitry. I have one with me. I believe that the Doctor's specialized skills might enable us to ascertain the truth and possibly devise a solution more quickly than I would be able to do on my own."

"Understood," Janeway said. "We'll send him right down."

"Acknowledged," Tuvok said. "You may also wish to find out what happened to the others who were assigned to this area. It might have a bearing on my current situation."

"We're on it, Tuvok," Janeway said. "Good work."

"We shall see, Captain," he said. "The work is not yet complete. Tuvok out."

Static replaced his voice, and then Paris cut the link.

"Wow," he said. "That was brilliant. I'm not sure I would've thought of that."

"Tuvok seems to be waging his own little war down there," Chakotay said. "Let's hope he can continue."

"Is there any way of finding out what happened to the staff?" Janeway asked.

"Not without the computer's help," Paris said, "and I doubt we'll be getting that."

"It's possible the computer created an emergency, or even a false one, in order to get the crew out of engineering," Chakotay speculated. "To keep them from doing exactly what Tuvok's attempting now."

"Ensign Gilbert," said Janeway. "See if you can find out who was assigned to that area during this shift and try to reach each of them by combadge." Janeway turned back to her first officer. "How long do you think Tuvok has before the computer takes action?"

"Hard to say," Chakotay said. "It thinks faster than we do. But it's not thinking consistently."

"What do you mean?"

"Think about it. The computer wants to kill Seven, but it could have done that just by destroying the Rhawn ship. Instead, it takes potshots at relatively low power. Then when you try to give it orders, it ignores you, until you ask it a direct question. And after a few minutes of that, it ignores you again."

"What are you suggesting?" asked Janeway.

"I think the computer is conflicted," Chakotay said. "Whatever was done to it either wasn't finished, or it isn't able to completely override the redundant safeties in its programming."

"You think the computer is fighting itself?" Paris asked.

"On some level, maybe it is."

"If that's true," Janeway said, "it may give us a better chance of getting through this. Continue working on the computer up here, and make certain that you're obvious about what you're doing. The more we can draw its attention away from engineering, the better."

Chakotay nodded.

Janeway walked toward her chair. "Mr. Paris, get down to sickbay and make sure the Doctor joins Tuvok. Use the Jefferies tubes."

"On my way," Paris said as he rose. He shook his head. "You know, the combination of the radio and the mad computer actually reminds me of a *Captain Proton* episode—"

Janeway looked at him dangerously. "Keep your mind on your work, Tom."

"Yes, ma'am," Paris said, and left the bridge in a hurry. Janeway settled into her command chair, feeling, for the first time, as if things just might go her way.

13 hours, 41 minutes

"Have we found the aliens yet?" Aetayn snapped.

Voyager had stopped firing on him, but he didn't know how long that would last. For all he knew, they could be reloading their weapons.

"We have received word that two of them are trapped in our engineering unit," said Erese.

"Good," Aetayn said. "Let's bind them, then get some images of them, and send them to Janeway. She will be less likely to attack when her own people's lives are at stake."

"Forgive me, Excellency," Iquagt said, "but she did attack our ship while her people were standing on its hull."

"Perhaps it's a trick," Gelet said.

"To what end?" Aetayn asked.

"A way of taking over our ship. Erese did say that the aliens were in our engineering section."

"And," Erese said, "before they arrived, their captain asked us to turn off our engines. We complied."

"What could they do in such a short time?" Aetayn said. "They have to get out of here as quickly as we do."

"Perhaps they need fuel," Iquagt said. He usually

170

wasn't part of these kinds of brainstorming sessions, thinking them for intellectuals and weaklings.

"Fuel?" Aetayn repeated, not certain what Iquagt's train of thought was.

"They might need something from our atomic engines—plutonium, perhaps."

"They have the capability of transferring the entire reactor core to their own ship," Erese said. "If they can transfer people through space, why not other types of matter?"

Why not indeed? What a horrible, terrifying practice. Finding a ship in trouble, and then playing on its desperate need to fulfill *Voyager*'s own lack.

"Get those images," Aetayn said. "Let me know the moment we have them. Then I'll hail Captain Janeway."

Although he was beginning to wonder if his staff was correct. Would she be willing to sacrifice four crew members to save her entire ship?

Would he?

He didn't want to think about the answer to that, because it was obvious, and it was ugly.

But the truth rose to the surface quickly.

Of course he would.

13 hours, 40 minutes

Tuvok worked as quickly as he could. He felt sweat trickle down the back of his neck. He suspected the computer was tampering with the environmental controls in engineering—a simple feat, part of the basic functioning that he had to leave on. The computer was doing what it could to thwart him.

However, he was working in such a way that it did not know exactly what he was trying to do.

At least, that was his intention. The difficulty was that the computer also used logical reasoning in determining what it needed to know. There was a chance, an 87.5 percent chance to be exact, that the computer would figure out what he was doing.

Tuvok glanced over his shoulder. He wondered if the Doctor had been notified yet, and if so, whether or not he was on his way to engineering.

Tuvok heard a faint sound behind him. He turned, and saw only the empty engineering bay, the stations that had no crew members, and the continued pulsing of the warp core.

He examined the console he was working on. The computer did not seem to be resolving the problems he had set up to trap it. Its energy seemed focused elsewhere.

The sound came from behind him again. Faint, almost an echo. He studied the computer display, saw a heat spike in the trilithium resin storage tanks. Trilithium resin was the extremely toxic waste by-product created by the matter-antimatter reaction in the warp core. The resin was highly unstable. Adding heat to the by-product would only make its interior reaction worse.

The trilithium resin storage tanks were designed to take an inadvertent explosion. But Torres had informed the senior staff just two weeks before that they would soon need to find a place to dispose of the resin, because *Voyager* currently had twice as much as the recommended amount in their tanks.

Tuvok processed all of this information quickly.

An explosion in the trilithium storage tanks would not destroy *Voyager*, but it would send the toxic matter all over the ship.

The only way the crew members would survive such an event would be to seal off engineering and vent the resin and the resultant fumes into space.

Tuvok tried to create a forcefield around the storage tanks, but of course the computer did not respond. It had been lurking, waiting for him, letting him work to distract him.

He hit the communications part of the board, wondering if the computer would let him tell the captain what was happening. Of course, he got no response.

Then Tuvok tried to seal off engineering. He couldn't do that either.

And all of his work on the computer had been for nothing. The computer had monitored his every move and countered it, like an excellent chess player. Only, unlike a chess player, the computer had kept its moves hidden.

Tuvok tried one last thing. He tried to bring down the temperature in the storage tanks manually.

The computer froze him out of the controls.

If he stayed in engineering when the tanks blew, he would die. He estimated that he had two minutes and fifty-two seconds to find a solution or to get far enough away from engineering that the initial explosion would not affect him.

The explosion might cause problems with the warp core, however. He set up a forcefield around it, and the computer let him do that. He tried once again to set up a field around the storage tanks and the computer blocked him.

It was, at best, a stalemate.

But there was a 97.8 percent chance that the computer had defeated them all.

13 hours, 39 minutes

Tom Paris ran through the corridor toward sickbay. He had never climbed down a Jefferies tube so fast in his life. The doors to sickbay were open, but there were no patients inside. The biobeds were empty and the Doc's office was empty as well. Opera played overhead—some woman was screeching loud enough to make Paris's ears hurt—but the Doctor was nowhere to be found.

"Doc!" he shouted. "Doc! Computer, activate EMH."

He braced himself for the Doc's fussy greeting: *Please state the nature of the medical emergency.* But it never came.

"Computer," Paris said as a reflex. "Turn off the music."

And, strangely enough, it complied.

The silence actually echoed. He could still hear that woman's high-pitched vibrato in his ears.

"Computer," he said, wondering if maybe all the control functions had moved to this room, "restore full computer control to the bridge."

"Warning," the computer said in response, but it didn't continue. Usually the computer explained the nature of the warning.

"What warning?" Paris asked.

"Warning," the computer said again, and he could swear he heard a chuckle in its voice. He knew that

174

wasn't possible. It was his imagination—it was chaotic. And while he thought of the computer as the villain of the piece, its utter lack of emotion made that role, at least as he imagined it, impossible.

"Computer, activate EMH," Paris said again.

"Warning," the computer intoned. "Life-support will cease in one minute and thirty seconds."

"Nice of you to share that." Paris refused to panic. He knew that even after life-support failed, the ship would remain habitable for hours, even days in some areas.

He walked around sickbay, looking for the Doctor's mobile emitter. Nothing.

Paris cursed softly. Without the Doc, Tuvok might not be able to save them.

13 hours, 38 minutes

"Warning," the computer said again. "Life-support will cease in one minute and thirty seconds."

The computer's voice sounded a little odd somehow, almost unknowable, as if a stranger was speaking for it. Which, Janeway supposed, was exactly the case. "Looks like you were right about the computer being conflicted, Chakotay," she said. "Why else would it suddenly decide to warn us? What have you found out?"

"Not much," Chakotay said. The bridge seemed even emptier without Paris there, as though each member of her senior staff were disappearing one by one. Something suddenly appeared on Chakotay's panel. "Captain, I'm getting that radio signal again."

Tuvok. Janeway waved a hand. "Let's hear it."

"Captain." Tuvok's voice sounded tinny. "The computer is raising the temperature in the trilithium resin storage tanks. I have tried to compensate, but I do not seem to be making progress. Do you know where the Doctor is?"

"Mr. Paris has gone for him. If those tanks rupture, Tuvok, you won't survive."

"I am well aware of that, Captain. I will have, at most, fifteen seconds to vacate my position."

"He's right," Chakotay said. "Those tanks are much too hot."

"You can read that?" Janeway asked.

"The computer is letting me see and do several things that it wasn't allowing a few moments ago."

"It has been monitoring us all along, Captain," Tuvok said. "I will do my best to solve this crisis, but you needed to know what was about to transpire."

"Captain," Chakotay said, "I don't know what he plans on doing, but that resin is so unstable, and at these temperatures, it might not give him any warning before it blows."

"I'm fully aware of that, Chakotay." Janeway took a deep breath. "Get out of there, Tuvok. Do you hear me? That's an order."

"He severed the radio link," Chakotay said.

Damn Vulcans. Always so heroic. "Chakotay, can you seal off engineering if those tanks rupture?"

"The computer is giving me access at the moment, Captain, but I don't know how long it will last."

"Do you have a reading on Tuvok? We can beam him out of there."

"According to his combadge signal, he's in the computer core."

Janeway let out a sigh. Of course. Tuvok had taken off his combadge to fool the computer. "Can you get a reading on his lifesigns? He says he's the only person in there."

"Warning," the computer said. "Life-support will cease in sixty seconds."

"Why is it warning us?" one of the ensigns asked. Janeway heard panic in his voice.

"Good question," Janeway said. "Chakotay? Tuvok's life signs."

Chakotay shook his head. "Captain—"

Suddenly klaxons sounded all over the ship, and the red alert notifications went off even though Janeway hadn't ordered them.

"The tanks have blown," Chakotay said.

"Blown?"

"Aye, Captain."

"What about the warp core?"

"Undamaged at the moment, but the toxins are spreading all over engineering."

"What about Tuvok?"

"I can't find him, Captain." Chakotay sounded upset.

At that moment, the life-support systems failed. The bridge went black, then the emergency lights came on.

"We could have used a warning on that," Janeway mumbled.

"I think our warnings are done," Chakotay said.

"What do you mean?"

"I mean that the computer has turned on the fans in engineering. The toxic vapor will spread all over the ship in a matter of—"

"Warning," the computer said. "*Voyager* will be unsuitable for Class-M life in ten minutes."

"We got that," Janeway snapped, although it would do no good. "Commander, can you turn those fans around, vent this material into space?"

"On a good day, sure," Chakotay said, his fingers flying over the console. "I don't have to tell you that this is not a good day."

"Great," Janeway said. Her choices were poor ones. Either she had to find a way to stop this computer and vent the toxins in less than five minutes or she had to find another way to save her crew.

"Chakotay, can you get me shipwide?"

"Strangely enough," he said, "I can."

She figured as much. It was exactly what the computer wanted. "Do it."

"Done," he said.

"Attention all hands. This is Captain Kathryn Janeway. Abandon ship. Repeat. Abandon ship. The crew will rendezvous on the engine pod of the alien ship *Traveler*. This is not a drill. Repeat. This is not a drill."

"Captain—" Chakotay started, but she waved her hand at him, silencing him.

"That goes for the bridge staff as well," she said. "Repeat that announcement. Make it continue as long as we're on ship. Everyone knows their evacuation orders. Follow them."

"Captain," said an ensign. "What about the Rhawn? What will they do?"

Janeway didn't answer, but the question hung in the air. What *would* the Rhawn do when they found themselves invaded by all of *Voyager*'s crew?

And in just over thirteen hours, unless they found a solution, all eight hundred million of them, plus her entire crew, were going to die.

"Captain, request permission to stay aboard and see if I can shut down the computer," Chakotay said.

"Request denied. I said to abandon ship, and I mean everyone." Janeway took a deep breath. "Even me."

Chapter Eight

13 hours, 38 minutes

It was perhaps the most ridiculous thing Seven of Nine had ever seen. Two Starfleet officers held at bay by several men with knives. Granted the men with knives were larger, but Harry and Vorik wore phasers. One shot, and the men would no longer be a threat.

Initially, Torres had whispered to Seven that there must have been some kind of threat that the two of them didn't yet understand. But the longer Seven watched, the more she did not believe that.

It wasn't even as if the Rhawn men were that talented with their knives. They held the knives incorrectly, for one thing, gripping them in a way that allowed them no leverage. For another, they did not move them in a menacing fashion.

With a single kick of his foot, Harry could get

free. Vorik was another matter. Perhaps he did not
think it logical to kick someone holding a knife.

Seven and Torres hadn't yet been noticed by the
crew holding Harry and Vorik. Torres had quietly
closed the door behind them so that the students,
their teacher, and that annoying engineer did not follow them in. Not that they would have, anyway.
They seemed quite appalled that Seven and Torres
had entered this area.

Rules of behavior among the Rhawn were appar-
ently designed to restrict movement within the ship.
The inhabitants took them very seriously, something
Seven felt she and Torres could use to their advantage.

A piece of equipment chirruped behind the men.
One of them cursed—at least, Seven believed that
comment about ancestors and mud holes was a
curse—and shoved another man over to take his
place. Then he went toward the chirruping equipment.

Four men guarded Vorik and three guarded Harry,
and still neither of them made a move. Seven could
hear Harry's voice, but she couldn't make out the
words.

The poor boy was probably trying to talk his way
out of his predicament.

Seven had had enough. She started toward the
group. Torres caught her arm.

"We still don't know what's going on," she whispered.

"We know enough," Seven said.

She walked to the edge of the walled space, and
put her hand at her side. No one seemed to notice
her, even though she was only a few meters from
them.

Now she could understand Harry.

". . . really are allies. Just ask your emperor. We were working for you guys when we got attacked and had to jump through that conduit. It was . . ."

Seven cleared her throat. No one noticed.

". . . not an attempted invasion. If we were going to invade, we would have—"

"Mr. Kim," Seven said.

All of the Rhawns, even the one speaking into that strange piece of equipment, turned toward her.

"Why haven't you disarmed these primitives?"

The look of panic on Harry's face was worth the effort it took to get everyone's attention. "I can't, Seven. We're allies. They might take it wrong."

"I take their knives wrong." She faced the men. "Drop them."

One of the Rhawns grabbed Harry by the collar and pulled him close, pointing the knife at the vulnerable spot under Harry's chin.

"He's our prisoner," the man said, "just like you'll be."

"Doubtful." Seven thumbed her phaser control to Stun. "I give you one more opportunity to set down your weapons."

The Rhawns laughed at her. She did not like to be laughed at.

"Seven," Torres said. "Harry has a point. We are allies—"

Seven brought her phaser up and, in a single movement, shot the Rhawn holding Harry. His knife clattered to the ground as he fell backward, unconscious. Two of his fellows ran to his side. The others dropped their weapons and ran.

"Seven!" Harry ran his hand underneath his chin, then checked the palm for blood. "He could have stabbed me."

"It was a calculated risk," Seven said. "I did not believe it likely that you would have been seriously injured."

"Seriously injured? I don't like that criterion."

"You had your chance," Seven said as she came forward. "You should have taken control of the situation from the beginning."

"We were in control," Harry said. "We were just taking our time, trying to convince them that we're allies."

"You've ruined any chance of that," Torres said, but Seven heard a smile in her voice.

"I am not concerned with diplomatic relations. We must get to a command area and contact the captain."

The Rhawn who had gone to silence the chirruping equipment was holding a small piece of it in his left hand. He was watching the proceedings with growing dismay.

"Are we your prisoners now?" he asked.

"If you like," Torres said.

"Ah, jeez, we're really messing this up," Harry said.

"No." The Rhawn spoke softly. "We have already done that. Our emperor wanted us to hold you prisoner to convince your captain to stop firing upon our ship."

"The firing stopped a few minutes ago, pal," Torres said. "You have nothing to worry about."

"We disobeyed the emperor."

"Oh, of all things," Torres said. "You didn't disobey anyone. You lost."

The Rhawn stopped beside the three men who remained. The one Seven had stunned was just beginning to come to. "We are your prisoners now. What will you do with us?"

"Nothing," Seven said

Torres grinned. "Nothing difficult, that is."

Seven looked at her. Sometimes she found B'Elanna Torres extremely unpredictable. "What do you mean?"

"Meet our new guides, Seven. I think they can get us through this ship fairly quickly, show us the transportation system, and maybe some food along the way."

Seven raised her eyebrow. "An excellent plan," she said. "One guide for each of us."

"B'Elanna," Harry whispered loudly. "We're supposed to be allies."

"They attacked us first," Torres said. "And they were going to hold you hostage. Forget the allies thing, Harry."

"Where are we going?" Vorik asked. It was the first thing he'd uttered since the women had entered the room.

"To meet the emperor, of course," Torres said.

"He's on the other end of this thing," Harry said. "Two hundred kilometers away."

"We know," Seven said. "Which is why we must hurry and have guides for transportation."

Harry shook his head. "How did I know this was going to be a bad idea?"

"Enough discussion." Seven was feeling impatient. "We have a long journey ahead, and time is running out."

* * *

Tom Paris continued his frantic search for the Doctor's holo-emitter. He had no idea why the captain had issued an abandon-ship order. All he knew was that he was dangerously close to disobeying it.

The red-alert klaxons were sounding almost continually, and the computer would occasionally add an annoying *Warning* to the mix.

He began to wonder if the Doctor's holo-emitter, or worse, his very program, had been destroyed.

"Come on, Doc," Paris muttered.

Paris would take one last look in the doctor's office, and then he had to leave. If he died here, he had a hunch Torres would track him down in Sto-Vo-Kor or whatever their mutual afterlife would be, and make him suffer terribly for dying on *Voyager.*

. . . This is not a drill. Repeat. This is not a drill. . . .

He was just about to leave when he saw it, pushed up against the legs of the Doctor's chair. Paris let out a whoop of joy, scooped the mobile emitter into his hand, and ran for the door.

Fortunately there were a lot of escape pods near sickbay. He had a hunch he wouldn't have made it any farther than that.

13 hours, 30 minutes

Janeway didn't trust the computer to tell her when everyone was off the ship. She was using a tricorder, taking as many readings as she could. Chakotay had been helping her, until she ordered him to leave on one of the shuttles.

He'd been reluctant to go.

Decks were flooding with the poison from the ruptured tanks. She only had a few minutes left.

Tom Paris had contacted her from an escape pod. He hadn't felt he would have time to get from sickbay to the *Flyer*.

He had been right; he wouldn't have made it. But time wouldn't have been his problem. The toxin was already flooding the turbolift shafts and some of the Jefferies tubes between sickbay and the shuttlebay.

The spread of the toxin didn't make sense. It was almost as if the computer was directing it.

She had kept track of evacuating crew members by their combadge signals, having the tricorder check off the names as they left the ship. Her tricorder showed only fifteen people still on board *Voyager*—thirteen who were waiting for her in the *Delta Flyer*, herself, and one other.

Tuvok. In her haste, she had forgotten that he had taken off his combadge. That unmoving signal wouldn't be coming any closer, and if she waited any longer, she would doom herself and members of her crew.

She wasn't willing to do that. She wasn't done with the computer yet. Just because she was leaving didn't mean she wouldn't be back.

And when she came back, she would solve this once and for all.

She turned and sprinted for the *Delta Flyer*. Tuvok hadn't come. He had been in engineering when the tanks blew. The chances of his survival were slim.

As she reached the door to the *Flyer*, she stopped. She had to try one more thing.

She set the tricorder to read life signs, not combadges. And sure enough, there was still one on the ship.

It was moving toward her very quickly through one of the Jefferies tubes.

She doubted there would be enough time for him to get the tube door open and make it to the *Flyer*.

It had to be Tuvok, she knew that much. There was no one else it could be.

She entered the *Delta Flyer* and made a beeline for the cockpit. Then she had the *Flyer*'s transporter lock on to Tuvok's biosignature and beam him aboard.

Tuvok landed squarely in the center of the small crowded ship, on his hands and knees, still clutching a bioneural gelpack. For a Vulcan, he looked rather stunned.

"Welcome aboard, Mr. Tuvok," Janeway said. "Buckle in. I have a hunch this is going to be a bumpy ride."

13 hours, 29 minutes

The medical team from Unit 2 had Andra stabilized. They had given her fluids, claiming that was what a burn patient needed the most, and they had wrapped her in cold cloths, easing her considerable pain. She was on a pain medication as well and was doing better.

They said the burns weren't as bad as they looked.

Lyspa had never felt so grateful in her life. The team had moved on, but they had sent some of the other survivors back to her with a makeshift splint to carry her daughter. It seemed that the survivor who had burrowed through the debris at the front of the viewpark had gotten help from that end as well.

The debris had been cleared enough that they could all leave. The worst cases were being taken to an emergency medical center that had been set up.

They were getting out. They were free. Andra wouldn't die and Onsflet's sacrifice wouldn't be in vain.

Everything was going to be all right. Even the shaking in the ship had stopped.

For the first time in what seemed like a long time, Lyspa had hope.

13 hours, 27 minutes

Janeway piloted the *Delta Flyer* away from *Voyager* and toward the alien ship, *Traveler.* Her fingers moved swiftly over the controls. The *Flyer's* passengers were silent. Except for Tuvok, none of them had seen Janeway this angry.

Probably because she couldn't remember ever being this angry before. Her ship's computer had taken over, essentially divorcing her from *Voyager.* And what an ugly divorce it was.

But she would return.

She would regain control of *Voyager* and she would do it quickly.

She just needed a little help.

Tuvok slid into the navigator's seat beside her. Except for that moment of surprise, he seemed unruffled.

"How did you get out of there?" she asked.

He shrugged. "It is no longer relevant."

"Of course it's relevant," she said. "I'm curious."

"I diverted the computer's attention, and then left the way I came. Through one of the Jefferies tubes."

"So the computer flooded the nearby Jefferies tubes, hoping to catch you."

"Presumably." Tuvok didn't sound too concerned about it. "The toxin has now spread all over the ship."

That subtlety was the only way he could express concern. "You were the last to leave, Tuvok." She smiled at him over her shoulder. "I used a tricorder to read life signs."

"I would have been able to take an escape pod." Oh, so that was what was behind his cool tone. She had embarrassed him by catching him in that position.

Either that, or the surprise that he had actually shown had embarrassed him. She found nothing more humorous than an embarrassed Vulcan. It seemed to be one of the emotions they had the least control over.

"I doubt that, Tuvok," she said. "The last escape pod was jettisoned nearly a minute before I discovered you in the Jefferies tube."

He said nothing to that. The alien ship loomed in the viewport. Huge and vulnerable. Even more so now that *Voyager* had been crippled.

The next thing was to find out if Seven, B'Elanna, Kim, and Vorik were still alive. Using the *Flyer*'s sensors, it took her only a moment to locate them. They were very much alive.

She let herself take a deep breath; then she transported them into the main engine pod of *Traveler,* where the rest of the crew were gathering.

Janeway's fingers found the communications panel. She had to inform Emperor Aetayn of what was going on, and reassure him that the attack was the result of a malfunction, that she fully intended to help him once she regained control of her ship.

She hailed Aetayn and within an instant his image filled her screen. He looked as if he had aged years in the last few hours. His features were haggard and pale purple lines ran through the whites of his eyes.

"Captain," he said and there was no civility in his tone. "I understand that your people are invading my ship."

"I meant to ask your permission, Emperor," she said, hoping to placate him, "but there was no time. We've had a serious computer malfunction and we needed to regroup somewhere. *Traveler* is big enough to accommodate us in the short term—"

"Such an interesting ploy, Captain." He sounded weary. "What do you hope to gain? Are you going to steal our energy supply? After all, we won't need it in a few hours."

"I assure you, Emperor, we're not after your ship or your supplies. In fact, we intend to help you as soon as we resolve our own crisis."

He smiled. It was a bitter expression and she could tell how deeply disappointed he was. It was as if all hope had left him, now and forever.

"You can stop toying with us now, Captain," he said. "You've already wasted too many of our final hours. Leave us in peace."

"Emperor, we intend—"

"I've heard enough of your promises, Captain. Take what you want from *Traveler*. Except anything in the engine core. We plan to restart our engines and run them at maximum. We might not get out of range, but we're at least going to try."

"No!" Janeway said. "Don't do that. If you do, we can't—"

But Aetayn's image had vanished. And, try as she might, she couldn't get him to answer the rest of her hails.

"Most illogical," Tuvok said.

"I'm sure it makes some kind of sense to him." Janeway stood. But it seemed the emperor was leaving her no choice. She had to stop him and stop him quickly. "Lieutenant Ryzen, take the helm."

"Aye, Captain." Lieutenant Ryzen was a slender unjoined Trill whose homesickness for the Alpha Quadrant had driven the Doctor to distraction. He hadn't been able to find a cure for it at all. Finally Neelix had designed a holodeck program for her that seemed to calm her down.

Janeway had been grateful. Ryzen was one of her best officers.

"You'll beam Commander Tuvok and me to these coordinates." Janeway pointed at the controls, thankful that whatever had gotten into *Voyager* hadn't affected the *Flyer.*

Yet.

"Then on my mark, you'll beam us to these coordinates."

"Yes, Captain." No questioning, no strange glances. Just acceptance. Sometimes Janeway liked that best in an officer.

"Let's go, Tuvok," Janeway said.

Tuvok followed her to the *Flyer*'s two transporter pads. The other passengers had to press themselves against the various walls and bulkheads to make room. She had gone past the *Flyer*'s maximum capacity by a long ways. It was a tribute to Tom Paris that the ship flew as well as she did, even when her weight and speed were compromised.

Janeway stood beside Tuvok on the pads. "Energize," she said.

The command center was even larger than she remembered it from her first visit here with Neelix. She hadn't seen so many people, so much equipment—most of it big and bulky—and so much wasted space in any other ship she'd encountered during her long career.

The entire staff looked at her and Tuvok with surprise. They had arrived next to a large chair that was the emperor's place of power. He wasn't sitting in as she had hoped he would be.

Instead Aetayn stood in front of a giant viewscreen, studying the various pods and shuttles and the *Delta Flyer* as they made their way toward his ship.

Janeway walked up to him. Tuvok flanked her.

His guards ran in their direction, but were too far away to be of help.

"Emperor Aetayn," she said.

He turned, perhaps even more surprised than his people had been. But his expression changed quickly as he attempted to mask his reaction.

"Captain, I don't know what we've done to deserve this from you, but—"

"Have you ordered the engines to restart?" she asked.

"We are running the preliminary figures," he said. "We want to get them up to maximum capacity."

"So that's a no."

"Actually, it's a qualified yes. You see—"

She didn't give him a chance to finish. She grabbed his arm and hit her combadge. Tuvok, following her lead, grabbed his other arm.

"Lieutenant," Janeway said into the badge. "Now!"

The guards were running toward them, weapons— knives and some sort of club? how strange was that?—out. The fuzziness took over at that moment, and the guards disappeared.

Or, more accurately, Janeway disappeared, along with Tuvok and Aetayn.

They reappeared in the engine area, another cavernous space, only this time it was filled with *Voyager* crew members.

"Captain!" Tom Paris said as he walked over to her. "So glad you could join us."

13 hours, 22 minutes

Aetayn was in his own engine compartment. He hadn't been here in half a decade. It took days to walk here, and nearly as long to navigate the various sections, tubes, and corridors in his aircar.

Their device had gotten him here almost instantaneously.

And he was surrounded by all of the aliens. Some were blue and bald. Others had ridges on their noses. Still others had pointed ears. One woman even had metal above her eye and on her hand.

Where were his people? Why hadn't they stopped this invasion?

Even as he thought the question, he knew. They hadn't stopped the invasion because they hadn't had the capacity to do so. His father had banned powerful weapons from being brought onto *Traveler*, afraid that they would pierce the hull. Guards used clubs and started carrying knives a few years back when the crime problem started. But that was it.

Knives did not work against people whose powers resembled the magical stories of Aetayn's childhood.

"I demand that you unhand me!" he said to Janeway.

"And I demand that you countermand your orders to restart the engines." She seemed calm.

"He can't do that," said a woman with forehead ridges and an extremely intense manner. "It'll interfere with the computer program I loaded."

"I refuse," Aetayn said.

Janeway sighed. "Send some guards to the control area for this monstrosity. Make sure no one tampers with anything."

Then she let go of his arm, and raised her voice to be heard by all. "I'd like to see the members of my senior staff over here."

It was as if he no longer mattered. "I demand you send me back to the command center," he said to the dark man Janeway had brought with her.

"You will have to discuss that with the captain," the man said, rather formally, and then he walked toward Janeway.

In fact, no one paid any more attention to Aetayn. It was as if he didn't matter. It was as if he were unimportant.

It was as if he were as common as everyone else.

13 hours, 19 minutes

The engine area smelled like grease, and not the kind of grease that Neelix created when he was cooking. Machine oil or axle grease. She hadn't smelled that odor in decades, not since she was at the Academy, taking her classes in Ancient Technologies.

She wiped her hands on her uniform. Her staff was pushing their way through the crowd. "Hurry, people! We don't have much time here."

They managed to surround her even quicker then: Tom Paris, who was holding the Doctor's mobile emitter as if it were a prize; B'Elanna Torres, Seven of Nine, and Harry Kim still in their EVA suits; Tuvok; Neelix, who had what appeared to be tomato sauce along one cheek; and Chakotay, whose left sleeve was torn—probably from the rough way Janeway had pushed him toward the shuttle.

"All right," Janeway said as softly as she could. The senior staff huddled around her as if she were calling plays at a basketball game. "Here's what I know."

She quickly explained what was going on—how Tuvok had learned that the computer had taken over the ship and how, it seemed, the computer had somehow gone over the edge.

"I believe it's keeping *Voyager* at a set distance from this ship," Janeway said, "while it tries to repair the damage that Tuvok inflicted on it."

"You should have gone for the AI matrix core," Torres said. "Shooting a phaser at it might have saved us lot of trouble."

"I did the best with the tools I had, Lieutenant,"

Tuvok said calmly. "You were unavailable for consultation."

"The computer is working quickly," Janeway said, "so that it can regain full control. Once it does, it will carry out its directive."

"What directive?" Seven asked the question. She seemed unusually intense, almost uncomfortable. Janeway didn't blame her. Discovering you were the target of a crazy computer had to be disconcerting.

"P1/OR . . . something. The computer claimed— let me see if I can recall this correctly—that it was safeguarding Federation interests and eliminating threats to those interests."

"And it perceived me as a threat to those interests." Seven did not make that a question. It was as if she knew.

"Yes, for whatever reason. The computer wasn't making a lot of sense at that point." The entire staff had leaned closer as their interest grew. Janeway felt a bit claustrophobic. "It claimed that Ensign Roberta Luke had programmed this directive into its systems. There may be some truth to that, as the problem seems to have derived from a gel pack, which Ensign Luke specialized in before she died last—"

"May I speak with you alone, Captain?" Seven had her head tilted as she often did when she felt things were most urgent.

"In a moment, Seven."

"Now, Captain."

"When we finish, Seven."

"Captain, I believe what I have to say is relevant to the discussion, but I do not feel at liberty to discuss this with the entire staff. Only you should make that decision."

Janeway sighed. Seven could be extremely difficult. But, judging from her demeanor, she felt that whatever she had to say was extremely important.

"All right, Seven, but make it quick."

Seven took Janeway's arm, much as Janeway had taken Aetayn's, and led her behind some thick machine with blinking electronic lights. The rest of the crew was talking quietly, waiting for orders.

The senior staff watched Seven and Janeway.

Emperor Aetayn was wending his way through the group, trying to convince someone to listen to him.

"Captain," Seven said, "when I was with the Borg, we assimilated many Starfleet personnel."

Janeway nodded. "I'm quite aware of that, Seven."

"Then you also know that we picked up a great deal of knowledge about Starfleet and the Federation, including knowledge that isn't common among most of its personnel."

Janeway felt tension grow in her shoulders. "You know about this directive?"

"Not specifically," Seven said. "But P1/OR is a classification of directives used by only one organization: a small number of covert operatives within Starfleet, members of a little-known autonomous subsection of Starfleet Intelligence designated Section 31."

"Seven, what are you talking about?" Janeway said. "There are no autonomous divisions of Starfleet, and certainly nothing like what you're describing. The Federation would never allow—"

"The Federation," Seven interrupted, "for the

most part isn't even aware of Section 31's existence. Only a few within it are. But Section 31 has for the past two centuries acted independently of any other authority to seek out and identify potential dangers to the Federation. Once identified, these threats are quietly dealt with."

Janeway had gone cold. What Seven was describing was impossible—the Federation equivalent of the Romulan Tal Shiar or the Cardassian Union's Obsidian Order; amoral organizations in which espionage, sabotage, and assassination were all part of a day's work, in which the ends always justified the means, no matter how heinous. It was antithetical to everything Starfleet and the Federation stood for. Now Seven was asking her to believe that such a thing existed on behalf of that same Federation, and that it was the architect of their current crisis.

And even as she raged against the idea, Janeway knew she had no choice but to believe it. The vast repository of knowledge from which Seven drew was the same as any Borg drone up to the time she'd been separated from the collective. With each new assimilation, knowledge obtained by one was shared by all. And in all her time on *Voyager,* Seven had never lied to her.

"Are you sure of this?" Janeway asked, unable to raise her voice above a strained whisper.

"Yes," Seven said. "I realize this comes as a disquieting revelation, Captain, but I assure you, Section 31 is quite real. I never mentioned it before because until now, the information was irrelevant to *Voyager.* I did not suspect the ship had an operative on board."

"Roberta Luke," Janeway said. "You're saying she was the operative."

"It would seem so," Seven said.

"She was assigned to the ship shortly before I received our orders to enter the Badlands. Was she sent to keep an eye on me?"

"We may never know," Seven said. "Given the timing of her assignment, perhaps her interest was in your mission against the Maquis."

Janeway shook her head. "And she wound up in the Delta Quadrant along with the rest of us. But why maintain the secrecy at that point? And why go after you?"

"What I believed happened was this," Seven said. "When *Voyager* found itself unexpectedly thrown into the Delta Quadrant, Ensign Luke simply adapted to her new circumstances, maintaining her cover and remaining watchful of *Voyager*'s activities, possibly assessing them within the context of their future impact on the Federation. When I came aboard, she identified me as a potential threat. It was, after all, a calculated risk on your part, to disconnect a lifelong drone from the Borg collective and accept me into your crew, compelling me to join your journey back to the Federation." Janeway opened her mouth to protest Seven's characterization of her, but Seven pressed on. "I believe Ensign Luke wished to eliminate me without drawing suspicion to herself, and planned to enlist the ship's computer in that endeavor. She was a specialist in biorneural circuit technology. She encoded the genetic material in one of the spare gel packs with the P1/OR directive, a set of instructions to kill me and make it appear to be an accident, if possible."

"But she died before she could finish," Janeway said, following Seven's hypothesis. "And eighteen months later, B'Elanna swaps out that very gel pack, not knowing it's been tampered with. And that's when our troubles started."

"Precisely," Seven said, "And now that it has met with open resistance, the computer is doing whatever is necessary to carry out its directive. Do you see why I did not want to speak of this in front of the others?"

Janeway saw, but she was still struggling with what Seven had revealed to her. Finally she straightened her shoulders, affirming her resolve. "You made the right choice, Seven. Now we have to figure out how to solve this mess."

"I believe I know how to do that as well," Seven said.

Janeway raised an eyebrow. "Oh?"

"Essentially, Ensign Luke used a genetically encoded gel pack to take over the ship. I suggest we do the same."

Janeway recalled the gel pack Tuvok had come away with, and let out a small breath of air. All the tension went with it. "Seven, you're brilliant."

Seven nodded her head, as if acknowledging something she already knew.

"Come on," Janeway said, taking Seven's arm this time. "Let's go rescue our ship."

Chapter Nine

"Please state the nature of the medical emergency."

Oh, how he hated those words. They came out of his mouth before he even had a chance to think, before he could stop himself. But he kept trying.

Just as he'd tried now. When he reappeared in—

What? Some twisted crew member's holodeck version of the Dark Ages?

The Doctor blinked and closed his mouth, knowing that there was no medical emergency. The way the entire staff circled around him, he knew he had accidentally deactivated, but he didn't know how.

The last thing he remembered was updating patient files and asking the computer to choose a version of *The Marriage of Figaro* that used traditional instruments in the orchestral part.

Now he was in this dark, dank warehouse of a

place, filled with *Voyager*'s crew and a few tall skinny purple people who had to be the Rhawns. He hadn't seen Rhawns before, not in person, and he decided that through the viewscreen was a better way to be introduced to them.

"Doc!" Tom Paris clapped him on the shoulder. "Thank God you're back."

"You wouldn't be here without Tom, Doctor," Torres said. "He searched everywhere for you."

"And just where would I be if I hadn't been 'rescued'?" the Doctor asked.

"Still on the floor of your office, in the mobile emitter's matrix, all alone except for an insane computer," Paris said.

"Insane computer?"

"I suspect your backup program may have been deleted." This from Captain Janeway, who sounded remarkably calm about it.

"Deleted? *Deleted?* What idiot allowed that to happen?"

"Actually," Tuvok said, "I may be the reason it occurred. The ship's computer caused an overload in an EPS relay in an attempt to kill me. If I'm not mistaken, the relay ran through the computer core's holographic control circuits."

"Kill you?" The Doctor could hear hysteria in his voice, which he did not like. "Why in heaven's name would it want to kill you?"

"It tried to kill all of us, Doctor," Janeway said. "Or part of it did, anyway. We think the only reason it didn't succeed is that it may be suffering from something of a split personality at the moment."

"This is making less and less sense, Captain." He

glanced around. Some of the purple people were staring at him as if he had grown another head. He decided to ignore then.

"One of the bioneural gel packs has been tampered with," the captain said. "The sabotage has spread to the entire ship, through the bioneural network."

"By whom?"

"Ensign Roberta Luke. Do you remember her?"

Of course he remembered her. He remembered everyone who died on *Voyager.*

Severe rupturing of her arterial pathways. Internal hemorrhaging. Cardiac arrest. Complete collapse of her entire circulatory system. She died in agony, the Srivani's damned experiments taking their toll, testing her to destruction. And I was helpless to stop it.

Hers was one of the many faces he saw at night just before he shut his program down. Now the captain was telling him she'd been the cause of their current troubles.

One of the tall, thin purple people, a youngish-looking male, frowned and crossed his arms. He seemed very irritated.

His irritation irritated the Doctor. The Doctor wanted to be the only irritated person in this room at this moment.

"Doctor." The captain went on. "We need you to find a way to reverse what Ensign Luke did. Can you isolate what was done to it and devise a counterprogram to resequence *Voyager*'s bioneural circuitry?"

"With what?" he snapped, looking around. "Stone knives and bear skins?"

The tall, thin, young purple person flushed an even darker purple. Apparently the Doctor had offended him. Good. The Doctor felt like offending people.

Tuvok came forward and held out what was very obviously a bioneural gel pack, albeit a little singed around the edges.

The Doctor looked at it skeptically, but took it. "What about lab equipment?"

"We have the *Delta Flyer*," Seven said. "Its equipment is not as sophisticated as that of sickbay, but it will have to do."

The Doctor rolled his eyes. "All right. First I'll need to figure out what was done to the bioneural material, then see if a cure is even possible. Assuming it is, how do you plan on getting it back on the ship?"

"Worry about your end, Doctor," Janeway said. "We'll figure out the rest."

The Doctor nodded, then glanced at Mr. Paris and Mr. Kim. "Gentlemen, come with me. I need untainted genetic samples to use in my tests and you two seem to be the perfect donors."

They both moaned, which made him feel a little better.

12 hours, 16 minutes

Aetayn rubbed his nose with his thumb and forefinger, feeling the muscles in his face relax. He had misjudged the aliens. He had thought they were scamming him when they had been telling him the truth all along.

They were in trouble, and he had acted uncharitably toward them. He would have to apologize to Captain Janeway, even though the thought made him shudder. Emperors never apologized. That was his father's first and most important rule.

But his father had never been confronted by anything like this.

The group of aliens that Janeway called her senior staff had focused on a small device for some time, tweaking it with a long tool, and then they had proclaimed victory. At that moment, the surly man appeared, the one who believed he and he alone knew how to fix the ship.

The others seemed to believe it as well.

Aetayn was confused by all of this. He didn't know if the surly man, known as the Doctor (because of his medical or engineering skills? or was it just a nickname?), was really a man who had "beamed in" as the others had, or was some sort of mechanical being, or was some sort of god.

He wasn't about to ask.

He decided to let the aliens resolve their problem, and then, maybe, they would be able to resolve his. He had a few requests: He had to speak to his people before they tried something foolish against the aliens. He had to let his people know he was all right.

Surely Captain Janeway would understand the wisdom of that.

She had to.

11 hours, 51 minutes

Emperor Aetayn had apologized, of all things, and had asked to speak to his people. Janeway let him. She had other things on her mind.

Janeway could feel the precious seconds ticking

away. Every moment they spent on this ship was another moment lost in trying to save it. Her mind was reeling from a number of things, including Seven's revelation. Janeway didn't want to believe that elements within Starfleet employed methods that the Federation maintained were unacceptable. Janeway wondered what the effect of the shock waves created by this discovery would be, if she had the opportunity to convey it to Starfleet Command. Or was it possible that Command itself was compromised by Section 31, as her own ship had been? Could she even risk revealing what she knew, if she wasn't sure about the loyalties of the listener?

The thought made her furious. Starfleet—*her* Starfleet—was about idealism and trust, open-mindedness and truth. If Seven's description was accurate, Section 31 seemed to be able to exist as it did by exploiting those qualities as weaknesses. They acted for the Federation but without regard for what it stood for, as if those things didn't matter.

She hated what she was feeling. She wanted to lash out at something, anything. But there were other, more immediate, more important issues she had to deal with now. Section 31 could wait.

She had to get aboard *Voyager,* and quickly.

The Doctor had succeeded in isolating the genetic sequences in the infected gel pack that contained Ensign Luke's program. He'd seemed optimistic about creating a resequencing program that would cure the infection, essentially acting as an antivirus.

"Doctor?" she asked. "How are you progressing?"

"Much slower than I would be if you didn't nag

me every five seconds," he snapped.

Chakotay grinned at her, then shook his head. No matter how serious the crisis, some things always stayed the same—and one of those things was the Doctor's bluntness.

"Captain," Chakotay said, "I think I know how we can retake *Voyager.*"

She leaned wearily against a wall. "I'm listening."

"I don't think we can risk beaming anyone aboard; chances are, even if the shields are still offline, the computer may still be able to affect the beam, maybe set up a scramble field. But if we launch all the shuttles and the escape pods against *Voyager* to keep the computer distracted, it may be enough to allow one pod close enough to dock, so one of us, carrying the gel pack, can enter the ship. One of the docking ports isn't far from a gel pack bank."

"I know exactly where that is," Torres said. "I'll need to crawl through a Jefferies tube—"

"Don't get ahead of yourself, B'Elanna," Janeway said. She turned back to Chakotay. "All this is well and good, Commander, but the ship's sensors will register the pod docking."

"Perhaps not, Captain," Tuvok said. "In my opinion, the computer has not attacked us as effectively as it would have if Ensign Luke's sabotage were complete. Its errors have been significant, and response time poor. If its artificial intelligence is truly conflicted, as you and the commander have suggested, it may not be able to react to the pod before it's too late."

"You're not certain, though."

"I must admit that at the time I formed my opinions, I was more concerned with my own safety than with an in-depth analysis of the computer's reactions."

"Perfectly understandable, Mr. Vulcan," Neelix said from beside him.

Tuvok stiffened slightly, the Vulcan equivalent of rolling his eyes. Janeway smiled.

"I suspect you're right, Tuvok. That would explain the ease with which we vacated the ship. Doctor, I'm nagging. How soon will you finish?"

"Soon, Captain. This is precision work."

"If you don't hurry, Doctor, then all the precision will be wasted. Those suns are going to collide and there's no way anyone on this ship will survive without *Voyager*—"

"I am working with inferior materials," the Doctor said. "I would go quicker, but I do believe I only have one shot at getting this right."

"I don't like being called inferior, do you, Harry?" Tom Paris asked.

Kim grinned. "Doc, you want us to find you another donor?"

"Will you all stop annoying me?"

Kim's grin grew. Janeway resisted the urge to smile too. "Let's give him his moment," she said. "When he's done, I'll take that the gel pack into the pod."

"I'm the best person for the job, Captain," Torres said, instantly trying to convince her to not go. "After all, I'm the one who caused the problem in the first place."

"The person who caused the problem in the first place is dead, Lieutenant," Tuvok said. "That you used materials she had altered without your knowledge does not reflect badly on you."

"Thanks, Tuvok," Torres said. "But I still think I'm the best person for the job."

"I'm always leery of the captain doing the heavy lifting," Chakotay said. "You should remain in charge."

"No, Chakotay, you'll lead the 'attack,'" Janeway said. "Besides, the captain always goes down with her ship. If I fail, we're all going down in a few hours, along with the millions on *Traveler*."

The decision was made. She had used the decisive tone on purpose. The staff knew better than to contradict her.

"Actually, Captain—"

All except Seven, of course.

"—this is a two-person job."

"I've made my decision, Seven."

"But you were correct, earlier. Eventually, the computer will know that you're there."

"The ships will distract it, Seven."

She shook her head. "The computer has shown remarkable focus in attempting to reach its agenda since the pack was inserted. If it believes you are trying to tamper with it, it will attack you no matter what is occurring outside the ship."

"She has a good point," Chakotay said.

"You'll need someone to go as backup," Torres said, clearly meaning her.

"I was not thinking of backup," Seven said. "I was thinking of a diversion. A distraction."

Janeway studied her. "Just what do you have in mind?"

"Me," Seven said. "If I am on the ship, the computer will attack me first, no matter what you're doing."

"It would be suicide."

"No," Seven said. "I believe I can beat the computer."

"It's not a game, Seven," Torres said.

But Janeway felt that Seven already knew that.

"I am not treating it as a game." Seven spoke softly. "The harsh reality is that if the captain fails, we will all die, along with the residents of this vessel. My presence will ensure the captain's success."

"I calculate a ninety-three percent probabilty that you will die on this mission," Tuvok said, "whether or not the captain succeeds."

"I do not believe that your odds are accurate," Seven said, and walked to the Doctor. "Doctor, your work does not have to be perfect. It does have to be finished."

"And it will be finished," the Doctor said. "If you and the others would just leave me alone."

Janeway looked at the Doctor, then at Seven. "All right, Seven," she said. "Let's get ready to get our ship back."

Chapter Ten

6 hours, 2 minutes

Tom Paris sat at the helm of the *Delta Flyer*, looking at *Voyager* looming before him. She almost seemed like an alien vessel, certainly not like his home of the past five years. He knew his reaction was purely psychological—the effect of having a different entity control the ship—but it felt real.

He just couldn't discuss it with Tuvok, who was sitting behind him.

All around the *Flyer* were the escape pods. Their internal guidance systems—as minimal as they were—had been modified to allow them to be remote-controlled from a central locale, namely, Tuvok's console.

The escape pods were empty—all except one, which had Captain Janeway and Seven of Nine inside. They had the bioneural "vaccine" that the Doctor had created. It had taken him nearly six hours to complete the work, grousing any time someone interrupted him.

It was the longest six hours Tom could remember.

Paris understood the Doctor's irritation; being asked to do the impossible quickly was worse than being asked to do the impossible slowly, but still the wait had been interminable. Part of Paris was convinced they'd all die aboard that primitive alien vessel, in that dank and smelly engineering section with the Rhawn emperor glaring at them as if they were an invading army.

Which, Paris supposed, was what they must have seemed like.

He wasn't so sure this plan would work. He was most worried about Seven going along. He understood her reasoning, but he thought she might be sacrificing herself for nothing. He had been stunned that the captain had allowed it.

He hoped the captain had something else up her sleeve. If she didn't, he had a hunch that Seven was doomed.

The other shuttlecraft moved into view. Chakotay was in charge of the so-called attack. He was in one of the shuttles, B'Elanna was in another. Paris had wanted her with him, but he had known that wasn't possible.

He just had a bad feeling about this whole plan.

"You are mumbling, Mr. Paris." Tuvok's long fingers covered his part of the control panel. "It is distracting."

Paris jumped. He hadn't realized that he had been

making any sound at all. "Sorry, Tuvok. I'm just worried."

"We are doing all we can."

"I know that. I just have a feeling that this is gonna go badly."

"Is your feeling based on anything realistic, or is it simple fear?"

"Well . . ." Paris hated challenging Tuvok, but since Tuvok brought it up. "I know you think that *Voyager* may not even notice us, but if she does, and she's found a way around the damage you did to her tactical control system, we won't stand up to her weapons for long."

"Do you have another plan, Mr. Paris?"

Paris sighed. He'd always hated that kind of argument. *Don't complain unless you can do it better.* That reminded him of his father, and he hated being reminded of his father.

"No," he said.

"Good. Then let's get into position."

They had just received the signal from Chakotay. The signal was silent—a light had been triggered on their control panel, just as it had in the other shuttles. They had decided on radio silence in the off chance that the computer was monitoring all space communications.

Position for the *Delta Flyer* was the same as all the other shuttles: directly in front of *Voyager,* keeping the computer focused on them. The pods were dispersing to *Voyager*'s sides.

Paris couldn't tell which pod carried the captain and Seven, and he was grateful for that. If he couldn't tell, the computer wouldn't be able to either.

The shuttles spread out directly in front of *Voyager*. "Now what?" Paris asked Tuvok.

"We wait, Mr. Paris."

Paris supposed he knew that. But he didn't like it. Chakotay was supposed to initiate a game of chicken with *Voyager*'s computer, using some kind of sensor ghost to make the computer think it had been fired upon. Paris hated sensor ghosts, and he didn't believe playing chicken with a Starfleet ship of the line was a good idea.

In fact, no matter how much Tuvok challenged him to come up with a better idea, he still thought this was a bad idea all around.

He flicked the image on the viewscreen to the suns, just so that he could focus on some other unsolvable crisis. They seemed closer than he thought they would be. They were stunning, though, with the ripples of bright orange energy bursting off them. He could just sense the growing power, the imminent destruction.

It rather galled him to think that after all this crew had been through they were going to die here because they had come to look at the pretty stars go through some strange astronomical anomaly. If he survived this, he would vote to stop making scientific detours. He was beginning to think the price of knowledge was too high.

"Mr. Paris," Tuvok said. "You are making my job extremely difficult."

"Oh, sorry," Paris said, changing the screen back just in time to see a brilliant light leave *Voyager*'s phaser array.

In the instant it took the light to reach him, he understood that *Voyager* was firing on him. The beam hit, and the *Delta Flyer* rocked with the impact. The shields weren't damaged, not yet, but Paris had built the *Flyer* and he knew she could take a lot of hits, even from something as powerful as *Voyager*.

"Looks like she found a way around the damage you did," Paris said, working to maintain the shields and the shuttle's stability.

"I have eyes, Mr. Paris."

Another shot shook the *Flyer*. Paris thought his teeth were going to rattle out of his head.

Shots hit the other shuttles. It was only a matter of time before *Voyager* turned its attention to the pods.

"Return fire!" Chakotay had apparently decided to break radio silence. It no longer mattered anyway. The computer knew they had arrived. "Her shields are still offline, so target the phaser strips. That's still our ship, and we need her intact."

Paris's hands had already found the weapons controls, ready to fire on his own ship. "I don't like this," Paris said. "Not one bit."

5 hours, 43 minutes

They hit *Voyager*'s hull with an audible clang that ran through the interior of the escape pod. Janeway winced, hoping that Tuvok was right about the computer's response time.

Although it seemed that most of the signs were there that the computer had managed to repair some the damage. Through the pod's portals, Janeway and Seven had watched as the shuttles took a pounding. Seven had stated the obvious only a moment before:

that the shuttles were not designed to withstand that kind of force.

It was up to the two of them now.

Janeway nodded at Seven. They both put on the helmets of their environmental suits. Actually, Janeway was wearing Torres's suit. Not a perfect fit, but it would do.

The suits would protect them against the trilithium resin and enable them to cut through *Voyager*'s hull.

Seven already had the hatch opened. *Voyager*'s docking port doors stood closed before them. Janeway entered her authorization code. Nothing.

"Seven," Janeway said.

Taking her cue, Seven of Nine drew her phaser and fired at high intensity upon several very specific points, cutting through the docking port's seals. The light from her phaser reflected in the protective surface of her helmet. When she was done, she braced herself against the threshold of the escape pod and kicked. Once. Twice. On the third kick, the portal fell inward.

Janeway adjusted her grip on the modified gel pack as she and Seven boarded *Voyager*. Torres had been correct. The Jefferies tube they needed was only meters away. Seven disappeared inside, and Janeway followed.

It was dark. She had forgotten that all the life-support systems were off, which meant that non-important areas had no lights at all. Seven turned on her wrist beacon, and the beam created an eerie campfire-like atmosphere.

They climbed downward. The computer didn't seem to notice them.

So far so good, Janeway thought, although she knew better than to get her hopes up.

Seven said nothing as she led the way. Janeway could tell from Seven's posture that she was on alert.

The computer had already proven itself to be sneaky. Anything could set off an attack.

Janeway just hoped it happened later rather than sooner.

They had several meters of Jefferies tube to traverse before reaching the gel pack bank. To get there required them to take a sharp left turn into another Jefferies tube. On the pod ride over, she and Seven had debated whether or not they would stay together at this point. Seven had believed that if they stayed together, the computer would figure out their ultimate goal.

Janeway believed that together was the only way they would resolve this crisis. It was also, she knew, the only way she might be able to save Seven.

Seven levered herself into the new tube. Janeway poised to follow when the red-alert klaxons went off. The sound was deafening in the tubes. There was no computer voice, though, following the sound, no warnings.

That felt strange.

Of course, the computer didn't have to warn itself.

Seven dropped the rest of the distance to the Jefferies tube opening and let herself out. Janeway followed. As she climbed out of the tube into the gel pack bank, she found Seven at the nearby computer terminal. She couldn't read Seven's expression through her helmet.

"It appears, Captain," Seven said, "that the computer knows I am here."

"That's what we wanted, isn't it?" Janeway said, pulling a gel pack from the bank at random.

"Not exactly," Seven said. "The computer has decided to get rid of me by destroying the ship. The autodestruct sequence has been activated. I believe the program was initiated the moment I entered the ship."

"How much time do we have?"

"Less than a minute."

Janeway cursed. She tossed the tainted gel pack aside and plugged in the Doctor's replacement. The altered bioneural circuitry would immediately start intermingling with the rest, latching on to the genetic material already in the network, resequencing it as it went.

Janeway moved closer to the console. The countdown appeared in red digital numbers on the side.

Twenty seconds . . . nineteen . . . eighteen.

Janeway couldn't believe it had come down to this—an untested program that might or might not work. If it failed, it would be a failure that cost over eight hundred million lives.

Sixteen . . . fifteen . . . fourteen . . .

"The new programming should be taking effect." The Doctor had explained to both of them that the resequenced circuitry was very aggressive.

Ten . . . nine . . . eight.

Janeway found herself holding her breath.

Suddenly the light changed and the countdown stopped.

"Computer, report ship's condition," Janeway said.

The normal computer voice responded. "All decks flooded with trilithium resin."

She and Seven leaned on each other, just for a moment, as if they both needed the support.

Janeway felt slightly disoriented. Part of her wanted the computer to apologize for all that it had put them through. But, for all its assistance, for all it did, it was not a sentient being. It probably had a record of what happened, but no memory of it.

And no emotional stake in it.

"Begin decontamination," Janeway said to the computer.

"Decontamination begun," the computer said. "Approximate time until completion, seven hours, twelve minutes."

"Start with the bridge and engineering sections."

"Complying," the computer said.

One crisis solved. She took a deep breath and tried to refocus her mind. It was time to move onto the next.

Janeway looked at Seven and said, "Now we just have to figure out a way to save *Traveler.*"

"We may not have the time, Captain," Seven said. She moved to a monitor and brought up the image of the two suns, now a single, bloated, bursting mass. "The stellar collision has already occurred. There may have been an unknown variable that threw off our projections, or perhaps it was another effect of the computer's sabotage. In either case, our timetable was wrong. The blast wave will reach us in approximately two hours."

Chapter Eleven

1 hour, 57 minutes

The aliens had taken pity on him and returned him to his command center.

Emperor Aetayn sat in his throne, his hands gripping the armrests. He was trying to memorize this place, this position—for what, he wasn't sure. He would be dead soon. The ship would be destroyed along with everyone aboard.

His entire civilization, what remained of it; and the aliens, who would die because they had come to his aid.

He was sorry he had doubted them. He had been wrong. He had tried to approach the crisis the way his father would have, and the attitude made him act inappropriately. He should have trusted his instincts. He should have done what he knew was right.

Strange to come to such conclusions at the end of

his life, when he couldn't change or do anything about them. But that was how things were.

He was trying to accept it.

Everyone else on his staff continued working, just as if nothing were about to happen. When the last few moments came, he would order them to stop.

There was nothing more they could do.

There was nothing more anyone could do. He couldn't even send his people into the lifeboats, because there wasn't enough time.

Even if there had been time, there was no place for them to go.

He wondered what his people had done to deserve this fate. Extinction. The word was so much more final than death.

He lifted his gaze toward the screen before him, and watched the suns. Big, beautiful, orange balls, once the givers of life to his people and their now-vanished world.

Soon the suns would finish their final dance and collide, ripping each other apart in the process and sending out a sphere of devastating matter, energy, and radiation that would melt *Traveler* as if it had never existed.

The givers of life would be the bringers of death. Somehow that was appropriate.

Aetayn leaned back in his throne, and watched, waiting for the end.

1 hour, 37 minutes

The bridge didn't feel like home.

It was empty, for one thing, and even though the

environmental controls were back on, decontaminating the trilithium resin that had invaded every part of the ship, the bridge did not look like the place where she had spent the last five years of her life. It seemed to have extra shadows.

Janeway shivered in spite of the warmth of her environmental suit. Seven had gotten the viewscreen working and on it were the two suns, so close that they looked like a single mass—the light and heat and nuclear plasma radiating off them in a giant reddish glow.

Janeway didn't sit in her command chair. It felt odd enough to be up on the bridge in an environmental suit; she didn't want to compound the feeling of strangeness by sitting in her chair like this. Instead, she stood near flight control.

"Computer," she said. "How soon until the bridge is clear of the resin toxin?"

"Environmental norms have been restored to the bridge and engineering," the computer said.

Janeway took out her tricorder and double-checked. No trace of the toxic stuff remained.

"The computer is accurate," Seven said, pulling off her helmet and looking at Janeway's tricorder.

"Forgive me if I don't trust it yet," Janeway said, wondering if she would ever trust her ship again. Or her crew.

She didn't want to think about that.

She pulled off her own helmet. The air smelled fresh and the temperature was perfect. It was her bridge, even though it didn't feel that way.

"Get a fix on Harry, B'Elanna, Tom, and Tuvok, and beam them directly here," she said to Seven.

"Then contact Chalotay, let him know what's going on. Tell him to stand by."

That was a complete understatement. They had to effect a rescue in an impossible length of time. But she was going to do it. She had promised the Rhawns, and she would fulfill that promise. An entire species wouldn't die because someone on her crew had been disloyal.

Harry appeared first, still wearing his environmental suit, his helmet tucked under his arm.

"—vacation planets," he was saying, "places you wouldn't . . ." His voice trailed off as he realized where he was. His entire expression changed from one of great openness to surprise.

Janeway smiled. "Welcome aboard, Mr. Kim."

"Captain, I was—"

"Flirting." Her smile widened. "I understand. But we have a lot of work to do. It's safe to remove your suit. Get to your station."

As she spoke to him, B'Elanna appeared. She stood in the middle of the bridge, looked around, and sighed deeply. "Isn't someone going to say 'welcome home'?"

"Welcome home," Seven said, in a decidedly unwelcoming tone. "We must get to work."

"Well, hello to you too," B'Elanna said. "Where do you want me, Captain?"

"Here for the moment," Janeway said. As she said that, Tom and Tuvok appeared. Tom was reaching forward, still hunched over as if he were sitting in a chair. Tuvok was hunched too, but apparently he figured out what was happening quicker than Tom did, for Tuvok didn't lose his balance.

"You should warn a guy before you do that," Tom said, picking himself off the floor. "I could have been making a tricky maneuver in the *Flyer* and crashed it against *Voyager*. Hey, wait! Who's flying her?"

"I made certain you were not doing anything important," Seven said. "And I have enganged the *Delta Flyer*'s autopilot, and instructed it to return to the shuttlebay."

"I'm always doing something important," Tom said as he made his way to his station.

"Yes," Seven said. "I have been to that bar of yours on the holodeck. It is quite important."

"We can argue about this later," Janeway said. "Right now, we have work to do."

"Nice to see the old girl's back on our side," Tom said.

Janeway shuddered in spite of herself. She hoped the old girl was on their side. The computer had been very good at tricking them. When this crisis was over, she would have all of the gel packs double-checked as well as anything else that Roberta Luke had touched.

Or anyone she had ever spoken to.

"Here's the plan, and we have little more than ninety minutes to make it work," Janeway said, making sure she sounded more confident than she felt. "We're going to position *Voyager* directly between the coming explosion and *Traveler*, six hundred kilometers off the engine section. Get us there, Tom."

"Aye, Captain." Tom immediately executed the maneuvers, and then he whooped. "She's listening!"

"Of course she is," Seven said. "We wouldn't have brought you back here if we hadn't succeeded."

Janeway ignored the crosstalk. "Seven, you and Harry work on getting the deflectors back online. Then configure the forward shields so that they form a wide cone with its point aimed at the coming energy wave. And I want all side and aft shields to extend that cone as far as possible."

"I get it," Harry said, as if the plan were a revelation to him. "We form a wedge between *Traveler* and the explosion. We deflect the energy wave away."

"Such a procedure will save only the engine and sixth section of the alien vessel," Seven said.

"I know that," Janeway said, pacing. She knew that the energy wave, once past the cone, would collapse back on the long ship like water flowing around a rock in a river. There had to be a way to keep it from reaching those other five sections. But the shields would just not reach far enough. "Seven, double-check, would you? I want to make certain our calculations are right this time."

"Let me run a computer simulation," B'Elanna said.

"Quickly," Janeway said.

"Our calculations are correct," Seven said a moment later.

"Yep," B'Elanna said. "That's what the simulation shows. Your plan will save the engine section and the last section of habitat pods, but not the others."

"The spillover," Seven said, "will destroy the main parts of the alien vessel."

"Damned if we do and damned if we don't," Tom said.

"Are they able to pilot that ship from the engine section?" Tuvok asked.

Janeway looked at B'Elanna. She was the one

who had spent the most time studying the equipment on *Traveler.*

But B'Elanna was frowning at her computer simulation.

"Photon charges," B'Elanna said, more to herself than anyone on the bridge.

Janeway knew instantly what she meant. Low-yield, shaped photon charges, set up in succession along the hull of the other five sections of *Traveler,* would help deflect the energy wave away from the ship.

"How many would we need?" Janeway asked.

B'Elanna looked up, surprised. Apparently she hadn't realized that she had spoken aloud. "Four per section at each junction point. One for each quadrant of the section. And the timing would have to be perfect."

Janeway nodded, a determined look on her face as she looked back at the viewscreen. "Then it will be."

Chapter Twelve

"Your Excellency."

Aetayn froze. He'd never heard that tone in Iquagt's voice before. His pilot, the man who had steered *Traveler* from the beginning, had been unflappable as long as Aetayn had known him.

Now his voice quavered, and he sounded defeated. Two words and the man's entire demeanor had changed.

Iquagt didn't even have to finish his thought. Aetayn knew what he was going to say, but no one else did.

"The suns have collided."

Aetayn wondered what the proper response was. "I know"? "Well, that's it then"? Or nothing at all?

He said, "Thank you, Iquagt."

They would all die together, politely, keeping to their stations, never speaking to one another, never getting to know one another, even though they had spent a decade at such close quarters.

Through the corner of his eye, he saw his staff struggle for composure. Erese put a hand over his face, his shoulders shaking with silent sobs. Gelet stood very still, as if by being perfect he would survive.

No one screamed.

No one collapsed on the floor.

No one made a scene.

If tears fell, they fell silently, or after the person had turned his back on Aetayn so as not to offend him in his last thirty minutes of life.

Aetayn supposed he should make some sort of announcement, say something placating. But if he made a shipboard announcement, then he would initiate chaos for these last few minutes. Better to let his people die in ignorance than to die in violence and terror.

There was nothing he could say to calm his staff, so he didn't even try.

"Your Excellency." This time, the speaker was Gelet. "We are being hailed, sir, by the aliens."

So Janeway had a good-bye speech. That didn't surprise Aetayn. She seemed resourceful in all ways. Of course she would do the right thing at this time.

"Put them on screen."

The image he received startled him. Janeway was on the bridge of her ship, but her helmet was off. Apparently, they had gotten rid of the poison. These creatures were amazing.

And, apparently, they would survive.

He was surprised that he felt no anger about that. They, at least, would carry on the memory of his race. He could ask no more.

"Emperor Aetayn," Janeway said. "Warn all your people to hold on and prepare for a very rough ride. The computer program we installed for our last attempt should help your steering thrusters some."

He shook his head. Their cultural differences were great. It was too bad that they would never get the chance to explore them.

"I've already decided not to burden them with this knowledge. The destruction of the ship will take but an instant, Captain. Telling them in advance would be cruel."

Janeway's lips thinned as if his comments had annoyed her. "You don't understand," she said, her voice cold and low. "We're going to save your ship. But it's going to be rough, and your job is to keep it all together. Do you understand?"

He did, but he was stunned. "Captain, how—"

"Warn your people," she said, and then she signed off.

Of course she did. If she was going to do anything, she couldn't waste time explaining her methods to him. He felt a strange elation that he instantly curbed. They weren't out of this yet.

But they had a chance.

"Gelet," he said, "I want a complete shipwide announcement. Link me in."

Gelet's mouth was open, his normally calm face a mask of terror and disbelief. "Can they do what they say?"

"If they can't, we'll die with hope in our hearts, which is much better than we've been feeling at the moment." Aetayn stood. "I want the entire ship on emergency standby, all medical personal standing ready. We're going to keep *Traveler* together. We are going to live through this."

"You believe that?" Erese's voice quavered. He hadn't moved his hand from his face.

Aetayn walked down the steps to take command of his ship. "I have no other choice."

11 minutes

Janeway was standing on the bridge, in command of her own ship for the first time in hours. The rest of her crew was back on board, beamed over from *Traveler* and the "attack fleet," crammed into the few cleaned areas in the ship. Even from the few places, they were making certain that everything ran smoothly.

Everything was in position. *Voyager*'s shields were back online, drawing power directly from the warp engines.

They only had one chance at this.

All the simulations showed that the photon warheads would keep the energy wave away from the ship if the explosions were triggered at one exact moment in time. A fraction of a second in either direction would mean failure, and *Traveler* would be torn apart.

"The photon charges are placed and ready," Torres reported. "The detonation is locked into the computer to coincide with the arrival of the blast wave."

"Double check it."

"We're trusting the same computer that kicked us off this ship," Paris said. "Is that such a good idea?"

Janeway had already thought of that, but there didn't seem to be another solution. She just hoped the Doctor's alterations to the gel pack had destroyed all of Roberta Luke's program. Otherwise, everyone—on *Voyager* and *Traveler*—would die very, very quickly.

She couldn't even tell her staff to begin on her mark. The computer was going to do it all.

"The sequence begins in less than five minutes," B'Elanna said.

Janeway returned to her command chair. As far as she was concerned that five minutes was five minutes too long.

She hated waiting.

9 minutes

The emergency medical treatment center was filled with people from the viewpark. Lyspa sat in a tent with Andra beside her. Her daughter's skin had returned to its normal color and she was sleeping. The doctor promised Lyspa that Andra's legs would have scars that could be removed someday down the road, but that was the only problem she'd have.

She'd live a long and happy life.

Lypsa silently told her dead husband that. His sacrifice hadn't been in vain. They were all going to be fine. The nurse had already sent a notification for Andra to be moved to one of the hospitals farther into the unit—one of the few that hadn't been damaged by the asteroid hit.

In a few hours, Andra would be asleep in a hospital bed, being tended by the very latest equipment, and this would all be a bad memory.

Then she heard a horn on the public address system, a horn that made her skin grow cold. No one had used that system since the first days after *Traveler* had left Rhawn.

"Stand by for an announcement from the Emperor."

The words were staticky and strange-sounding, spoken by an unfamiliar male voice.

Andra opened her eyes. "Mommy?"

Lyspa took her hand, unwilling to say everything was all right. The emperor hadn't made an announcement in all the years they had been moving away from their home planet. Everything was clearly not all right.

"People of *Traveler,* the event we have been waiting for, planning for during the last one hundred years, has occurred."

The emperor sounded so young. Lyspa had never heard his voice before. His father's voice had been harsh and commanding, almost frightening. This voice was warm and melodious. Caring.

"The suns have collided."

All around her, Lyspa heard gasps. No one had discussed the colliding suns in so long that many of them had forgotten it was going to happen. Lyspa hadn't. She had been wondering when this announcement would come.

Andra's hand tightened on her own.

"We did not make it as far as we had hoped, and we are in some danger—"

Voices rose in alarm. Someone shushed them.

"—the energy released from the collision. However, as many of you know, a group of aliens has been helping us—"

"Aliens?" Andra said. "Is he making this up?"

232

Lyspa shook her head and with her free hand put a finger to her lips.

"Thanks to them, we will make it through this crisis, but how well we will survive is up to you. We will have a rough ride. I want you to get into the open, stay there until I tell you everything is fine, and stay away from anything that will fall. Above all, you must remain calm. We now have a future. It is up to you to make certain it is a golden one."

And then the staticky sound disappeared.

There was complete silence after his announcement. Lyspa was holding her breath. She had thought they were safe. She hadn't realized what kind of threat they had been under. All along, she had been struggling to survive and they still might have died.

Except for aliens. Aliens?

"Mommy?" Andra said. "Shouldn't we get out of the tent?"

Of course. The ship would shake like it did before. Lyspa didn't want to go through that again. But she didn't want to die either.

She stood, grabbed the back of her daughter's bed, and wheeled her into the yard beyond. An orderly stood near one of the roads, indicating to people where to go.

Everyone was moving calmly, silently, just as the emperor had told them to do.

They all looked as stunned as she felt, and she could read on their faces the thought she couldn't voice.

They were all wondering if they were going to die.

Chapter Thirteen

1 minute

Captain Kathryn Janeway had to stand up. She was in the presence of something awesome, something that could not be faced from a chair. She had to face it on her feet, as she imagined David had faced Goliath.

The viewscreens showed the energy wave coming toward *Voyager* and *Traveler* like a hot, boiling wall, expanding out from the explosion in a giant sphere of destruction. On the screen it looked like a rolling wave of fire.

But with every kilometer from the explosion, the force of the wave lessened, consistent with the inverse-square law. However, it would still be strong enough when it hit *Voyager* and *Traveler* to vaporize them both if they were left unshielded.

"Thirty seconds," Chakotay said. He sounded as awestruck as Janeway felt. When she had said that she wanted to come close to this astronomical anomaly to study it, this had not been what she had meant.

"Computer standing by," Seven said.

Janeway's spine stiffened. She couldn't allow herself to think about the computer failing them. From this moment forward, if they survived, she would always question it when they put their lives in the control of the computer.

"Hold us in position, Tom," Janeway said.

"Aye, sir," he said.

"Fifteen seconds," Chakotay said.

The wall of fire and energy now filled the screen. She had never seen anything like it. It was as if the surface of a sun was rushing at them.

"Five seconds to impact," Chakotay said.

Janeway took a deep breath and held on to the rail as the wave smashed into them, flowing around them as if *Voyager* had just dove into a vat of swirling, yellow and red energy.

The impact threw Paris and Chakotay from their chairs. But she had been able to sway with it, move with it, anticipate it as she would anticipate the moves of a ship on an ocean.

She and *Voyager* were back in synch.

Then the shaking calmed and it was over.

"Report!" she said.

Tom pulled himself back in his chair. "The shields held."

He sounded ecstatic.

"Photon charges did their job." B'Elanna sounded surprised. Janeway was glad to know of Torres's doubts after the fact, not before.

"Damage report, Mr. Kim."

"Nothing major, Captain. A few bumps and bruises, some things falling. Pretty minimal." He bent over his console. He had one of the bruises. It was starting to form on his cheek. "However, there is extensive damage in all living environments of *Traveler.*"

"Is it holding together?"

"So far," Kim said.

Five minutes after impact

Aetayn held on to the back of his throne platform, his feet skittering beneath him as if they had a mind of their own. First the tremors had felt like waves, giant waves that he was riding as if he were surfing over them, and then they eased into vibrations.

His staff had fallen, screamed, yelled, and slid past him toward the viewscreens that miraculously still showed the space around them. For a while it had been filled with fire. Fire that had once lived in his sun, inside the star that gave them life, fire that was trying to take that life from them.

Then he couldn't watch as he struggled to remain on his feet. Somehow that seemed important to him, as if it were how he was going to regain his control.

The emperor could not be knocked down.

Equipment fell—his personal viewscreen, the one in front of his throne, toppled down and narrowly missed him, and behind him, he heard more than one scream cut off as something crashed.

But the vibrating was easing and the fire was gone.

He was still standing.

And *Traveler* was still here.

236

It was over. He knew it was over, and all that was left was the cleanup.

"Report!" he snapped in his own command voice. Not an imitation of his father's. His own.

No one answered.

They had to answer.

They had to focus on the future.

He turned around. Gelet was struggling to his feet.

"I need a report, now," Aetayn ordered.

Gelet nodded. He looked at his console. "We've got damage everywhere. Most of the juncture points show stress." He looked up at Aetayn, a light in his eyes. "None have separated."

"If they haven't separated by now, they won't." Iquagt said that. He was holding a bloodstained hand to the side of his face.

"Are there any hull breaches?" Aetayn asked, feeling frustrated that he couldn't look himself. The first thing he was going to do after this mess was cleaned up was learn how to fly his own ship. His father was wrong. An emperor did get his hands dirty. Any leader did, just as Janeway had done to save her people.

And his.

The silence after that question was too long for Aetayn's taste.

"Hull breaches?" he repeated.

"No," Iquagt said after a moment.

Aetayn let out a sigh of relief.

"We have casualties though." That voice belonged to Erese. He held a woman in his arms. She was a minor member of Aetayn's staff, so minor that, following his father's edicts, he had never bothered to learn her name.

And now she was dead.

Aetayn forced himself to look at her face, taking in every detail so he would never forget. "How many?"

"Two in the command center," Erese said. "There will be countless others in the units."

Aetayn nodded. He had known there would be deaths. They were unavoidable given the way that *Traveler* had been built.

"Make sure the emergency-services teams have full support. If they're needed in other units, make sure they can cross. Our first order of business is stabilizing the juncture points, so that we have a full complement of emergency services in each area. Can I make a shipwide announcement?"

"I'm working on it, Your Excellency," said a young man whose name Aetayn didn't know.

"Thank you," Aetayn said. He was about to turn away when he stopped. "What's your name, young man?"

The officer started, as if he were surprised that the emperor cared enough to ask him. "Pagedt."

"Good work, Pagedt," Aetayn said. "Good work, all of you. And congratulations. We survived."

Fifteen minutes after impact

The vibrating had slowed down to an occasional tremor. Lyspa held on to Andra. Her bed had collapsed, fortunately not injuring anyone. The tent had collapsed as well, and so had the few remaining buildings in the area, but thanks to the emperor's announcement, no one had been hurt.

People who had been thrown to the ground were

just beginning to pick themselves up. The hum of conversation grew all around her.

Andra threw her arms around her mother's neck and buried her face in her shoulder. Lyspa put her hand on her daughter's hair.

"I can't do this again." Andra's tears were hot on her skin. "Mommy, I can't do this again."

Lyspa tightened her grip on her daughter and rocked her as if she were still a baby. They had survived an explosion caused by colliding suns. Their home planet was gone. Their home sun was also now gone. They survived that. They could survive anything.

She had to figure out how to tell her daughter that. But she finally had more than enough time.

Chapter Fourteen

Ten hours after impact

Emperor Aetayn stood in front of his viewscreen, hands clasped behind his back. For the first time in the history of his people, they would be watching him on working viewscreens. Those who couldn't watch, or whose viewscreens were damaged in the explosion, would be able to hear his voice.

This was the first time anyone had done this, but he knew it wouldn't be the last.

The message he was about to broadcast would also be sent to *Voyager*. He had already expressed his gratitude, but he wanted to do it one more time.

The command center was still a mess of downed equipment. Many of his staff members had gone to be treated by medical personnel. Others had needed some time to check on their families and he had given it to them, something his father would never have done.

But Aetayn had finally realized that his father's way of ruling had not been a good way. It had resulted in a lot of misunderstandings, the destruction of families, and an isolation that had been crippling.

Some things he couldn't repair, but others he could. And the things he could change, he would.

"We're ready, Your Excellency," Gelet said.

Aetayn nodded. The official horn had been damaged, so Gelet made a simple announcement as he had the last time:

"Stand by for your Emperor."

Aetayn waited until Gelet nodded at him, and then he began.

"People of *Traveler,*" he said. He had liked that name when he used it before, and he liked it now. They weren't Rhawnians anymore. Not really. Rhawn was gone and *Traveler* was their world. It would remain their world until they found their new home.

Janeway had told him there was a planet several years away from him, one that would be perfect for their needs. She had already sent the coordinates to Iquagt. That, more than anything, had lifted Aetayn's mood.

"We have opened all the juncture points. Papers will no longer be necessary to cross from one unit to another."

Sadly, he was able to do that. As the death count rose, the precise balance of the units wasn't as important as it had been. One day it would become important again, but then he would have a different system in place to monitor weight and population, one that was much less restrictive.

"Medical personnel are to report to the necessary emergency sites. Hospitals should notify the command center of their damage, if any. We will continue to monitor the situation from here, and we will ensure that everyone who needs assistance will get it."

His people had assured him that was possible. He would make certain it was.

"In the past few days, we have survived two major crises. One would not have happened if we had had shields outside our ship that would protect us. Before this last crisis, our scientists started working on shields. Once our repairs are over, the shields will become our highest priority."

He would guarantee it.

"We would not have survived without the people of the starship *Voyager.* They have taught us many miraculous things. The first is that there is a universe filled with other beings out there, beings who can be kind and giving, even when it puts them in jeopardy."

He took a deep breath and went on. "*Voyager* put itself at risk to save us. They have shown us how to be citizens of the universe, and we shall do everything we can to follow their example."

He took another deep breath, partly to keep himself calm. He had learned a lot these last few days, mostly about the importance of tenacity and the importance of compassion. He needed both to keep his people alive.

"In the weeks ahead, we will share with you what we have learned about our neighbors in space, about this great alien ship, and about the universe around us. Knowledge will no longer be measured out to those deemed worthy. It is something we must all share."

Gelet was watching him, his expression stunned. Aetayn smiled.

"People of *Traveler*," Aetayn said, "we have embarked on a new era in our existence. We have survived the dangers of the past. It is now up to us to create a safe, peaceful, and healthy world for our future."

And with that, he signed off.

His entire staff was staring at him as if they'd never seen him before. His grin widened. They'd have to get used to the changes. It was time his people learned to think and act for themselves.

The crew of *Voyager* had done that, and by doing so, had been able to pull off a miracle.

He hoped his people would never need another miracle again, but if they did, this time, he wanted them to be prepared.

Epilogue

Two days after impact

Janeway sat behind the desk in her ready room, a cup of black coffee still steaming beside her hand. She was alone, staring through the windows at the stars beyond, wishing she could see all the way to the Alpha Quadrant.

She had just finished listening for the first time to log entries left by Ensign Roberta Luke. It was a secret document, meant not for her captain's ears, but for her unknown superiors back in the Alpha Quadrant. After a meticulous search through Luke's old quarters, Tuvok had found the chip hidden behind a ventilation panel.

Section 31, just as Seven had said. A secret, covert, autonomous agency within Starfleet itself. And it also appeared that Seven had been right about Luke's original mission: she'd been trying to gather intelligence that would help her group eliminate the Maquis.

Janeway felt stunned and out of breath, almost as if someone had hit her in the stomach. Until she had heard those log entries from Ensign Luke, Janeway had hoped that Seven had somehow been wrong.

But she clearly had not been. Section 31 was very, very real.

Janeway had bookmarked several sections of the log, passages that had both stunned and angered her. She keyed one of them now, listening once again to an entry made only weeks after they had arrived in the Delta Quadrant.

> . . . Janeway's acceptance of the Maquis into her crew has created a very high-risk situation on board, but so far I've seen no reason to act. On the other hand, if we succeed in finding a quick way to return to the Alpha Quadrant, then the knowledge these terrorists are obtaining about Voyager and Starfleet will be very damaging. If it does appear that a quick return is at hand, I may need to take more direct action to ensure that the Maquis never get a chance to use their knowledge. . . .

Janeway shook her head at the coldness in the words. Her memory of Roberta Luke was of a kind woman and a consistently professional officer, albeit a little distant and somewhat shy. But it had all been pretense.

Janeway keyed another log entry years later. Again Roberta Luke's voice came through clear and cold.

. . . If Janeway and her officers ever knew I
was on board, there's no telling what they
would do. They clearly have no inkling of the
larger picture they mess with almost every day
out here, trading knowledge for supplies, allowing aliens access to the ship, and not adequately gauging the future impact some of
their actions may have on the Federation.
Janeway shows potential enemies this ship's
abilities as if it's some toy to show off to a
friend. Sometimes I think I'm the only one on
board who still really cares about Starfleet and
the Federation. . . .

Janeway clicked ahead to the next log entry.

. . . I'm constantly faced with hard choices.
I knew that I would be when I agreed to this
life, as so many other patriots have. We do the
dirty work that needs to be done. We do the
work that lets all the citizens of the Federation
sleep in blissful ignorance of the threats that
we are constantly dealing with. Sometimes I
wish I could tell Janeway the truth, if only to
bang some sense into her . . . and she'd probably toss me in the brig, unable to wrap her
head around it. None of these people seem capable of understanding how much they need
people like me. The rest of the Federation is no
different. They all sleep like babies because
we're here, committing these sins so they
won't have to.

I never expected glory or recognition with this job. I'll go to my death knowing I did the right thing. That's all that matters. . . .

Janeway shook her head, disgusted and saddened at the same time. Roberta Luke, in her actions, had put the seeds of distrust throughout the entire ship.

Janeway especially had felt the seeds of it in herself.

At the captain's order, Tuvok hadn't read the log, and therefore knew nothing of what it contained. She had already told Seven never to speak of this. And yet, when she looked at the rest of her crew, she wondered.

Had someone gotten to Harry Kim?

Did the Doctor have a secret part to his program that made him keep tabs on the staff?

Was B'Elanna Torres as loyal as she claimed?

In the two days since Janeway had discovered that Section 31 existed, she had managed to shake some of those feelings. If there were other members in the crew, so be it. The traitor would be discovered soon enough, just as they had discovered Ensign Luke. They had disabled other Luke programs, set to boobytrap, just as the gel pack was, programs that hadn't quite been finished when Roberta Luke died.

But how many more were there? It would take Seven some time to discover that to the captain's satisfaction. More seeds of fear and doubt.

Janeway keyed one of Ensign Luke's last private log entries. It was dated just a few days before her death.

. . . Janeway's stupidity is apalling. Not only has she made a deal with the Borg, but she's

*brought on board a drone, cut it off from the
collective, and made a pet of it. What if she
can't control it? What if it reasserts its link to
the hive? What if it's already done that, and is
just biding its time so it can infiltrate the Federation and begin a Borg takeover from inside
Starfleet itself?*

*This has to stop. Now. I need to make only
a few more adjustments to the gel pack, install it, and the ship's computer will take care
of the matter for me. The threat will be gone,
and no one will ever know it wasn't an accident. . . .*

Janeway sighed wearily and killed the playback.
She stood and moved to the window, staring out at
the stars. Right now Section 31 was operating
throughout the Federation. She removed her combadge. It felt heavy in her hand. She turned it over
and over in her fingers, just staring at it.

The symbol on the badge meant something to her.
It symbolized everything she believed in, the very
things that Emperor Aetayn had praised *Voyager* for
to his own people.

How could there be a group willing to compro-
mise the ideals the Federation was founded on in the
name of protecting those very same ideals? The idea
twisted at her, made her even more angry, more set
on stopping this cancer.

It had to be stopped somehow. She could feel the
strength inside her come up, firming her resolve.
When she got home, Section 31 would not go un-
challenged.

She stared at her combadge and thought about all the good it represented. But what kind of hidden prices had been paid to achieve that good?

She wasn't sure she wanted to know.

Voyager would go on, but from that moment forward, the knowledge of Section 31 would follow her.

Like a shadow.

About the Authors

Bestselling authors Dean Wesley Smith and Kristine Kathryn Rusch have written over sixty novels each, and hundreds of short stories in different genres. Written under the name Kris Nelscott, Kris's novel *Dangerous Road* made the final ballot for the Edgar Awards for the best mystery novel of the year, while at the same time making the Edgar ballot for a short story written under the name Kristine Kathryn Rusch. Kris also writes wonderful fantasy romance novels under the name Kristine Grayson. She is also a Hugo Award and World Fantasy Award winner. Dean's most recent novel is the blockbuster novelization of the *X-Men* movie and a brand new *Spider-Man* novel. Dean has been nominated for every major award in science fiction and fantasy, and has won the World Fantasy Award. In *Star Trek*, besides writing with Kris, Dean has also written the *Captain Proton* novel, the original script for *Star Trek: Klingon,* and the very first *Star Trek: SCE* ebook, as well as books with two other authors. He also currently edits the ongoing *Star Trek: Strange New Worlds* new writer anthologies.

Look for STAR TREK fiction from Pocket Books

Star Trek®: The Original Series

Star Trek: The Next Generation®

Star Trek®: New Frontier

Star Trek®: Invasion!

#1 • *First Strike* • Diane Carey
#2 • *The Soldiers of Fear* • Dean Wesley Smith & Kristine Kathryn Rusch
#3 • *Time's Enemy* • L.A. Graf
#4 • *Final Fury* • Dafydd ab Hugh
Invasion! Omnibus • various

Star Trek®: Day of Honor

#1 • *Ancient Blood* • Diane Carey
#2 • *Armageddon Sky* • L.A. Graf
#3 • *Her Klingon Soul* • Michael Jan Friedman
#4 • *Treaty's Law* • Dean Wesley Smith & Kristine Kathryn Rusch
The Television Episode • Michael Jan Friedman
Day of Honor Omnibus • various

Star Trek®: The Captain's Table

#1 • *War Dragons* • L.A. Graf
#2 • *Dujonian's Hoard* • Michael Jan Friedman
#3 • *The Mist* • Dean Wesley Smith & Kristine Kathryn Rusch
#4 • *Fire Ship* • Diane Carey
#5 • *Once Burned* • Peter David
#6 • *Where Sea Meets Sky* • Jerry Oltion
The Captain's Table Omnibus • various

Star Trek®: The Dominion War

#1 • *Behind Enemy Lines* • John Vornholt
#2 • *Call to Arms...* • Diane Carey
#3 • *Tunnel Through the Stars* • John Vornholt
#4 • *...Sacrifice of Angels* • Diane Carey

Star Trek®: The Badlands

#1 • Susan Wright
#2 • Susan Wright

Star Trek®: Dark Passions

#1 • Susan Wright
#2 • Susan Wright

Star Trek®: Section 31

#1 • Cloak • S. D. Perry
#2 • Rogue • Andy Mangels and Michael A. Martin

Star Trek® Books available in Trade Paperback

Omnibus Editions
Invasion! Omnibus • various
Day of Honor Omnibus • various
The Captin's Table Omnibus • various
Star Trek: Odyssey • William Shatner with Judith and Garfield Reeves-
    Stevens

Other Books
Legends of the Ferengi • Ira Steven Behr & Robert Hewitt Wolfe
Strange New Worlds, vols. I, II, and III • Dean Wesley Smith, ed.
Adventures in Time and Space • Mary P. Taylor
Captain Proton: Defender of the Earth • D.W. "Prof" Smith
New Worlds, New Civilizations • Michael Jan Friedman
The Lives of Dax • Marco Palmieri, ed.
The Klingon Hamlet • Wil'yam Shex'pir
Enterprise Logs • Carol Greenburg, ed.